ME!

Published in the UK by Scholastic, 2025
Scholastic, Bosworth Avenue, Warwick, CV34 6UQ
Scholastic Ireland, 89E Lagan Road, Dublin Industrial Estate, Glasnevin,
Dublin, D11 HP5F

Text © Bethany Walker, 2025
Illustrations and cover © Katie Abey, 2025

ISBN 978 0702 34065 9

A CIP catalogue record for this book is available from the British Library.

Printed in UK
Paper made from wood grown in sustainable forests and other controlled sources.

FSC
www.fsc.org

MIX
Paper | Supporting
responsible forestry
FSC® C018072

10 9 8 7 6 5 4 3 2 1

www.scholastic.co.uk

For safety or quality concerns:
UK: www.scholastic.co.uk/productinformation
EU: www.scholastic.ie/productinformation

BETHANY WALKER

MEDUSA
GORGON'S
BAD
HAIR
DAY

ILLUSTRATED BY KATIE ABEY

MSCHOLASTIC

FOR CHERYL AND CAROLINE.
YOU ARE AWESOME.

PROLOGUE

DAY ALPHA

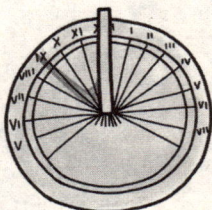

Dear Diary,

My name is **Medusa Gorgon** and welcome to the thoughts inside my head.

I've decided to write a diary because my best friend, Arachne, suggested it was something I might like. She's **SO** awesome – she just brought me these wax tablets and a reed stylus. So here I am giving it a go. What's the worst that can happen?

1

There's not a huge amount to tell you about myself. It's the usual stuff:

I have just turned twelve (I'm basically a teenager now!).

I have two older sisters, Euryale and Stheno, who are also GROSS, SCALY sea monsters. They too live in a cave. We don't have much in common.

I work for the goddess Athena as a guardian in her temple, and have done for the last three years.

I am MORTAL and HUMAN. This may sound like stating the obvious but, when it comes to my family, it wasn't guaranteed because...

I'm the daughter of sea monsters. Mum and Dad live in a cave on the coast.

I HAVE COMPLETELY AMAZING HAIR.

That last point may sound like a boast but it is the objective truth. I'm not sure my sketch does justice to my luscious locks.

But EVERYONE always comments on how lovely my hair is, so it must be true. I'm fairly sure it's what saved me from a life of cave-dwelling with my monstrous family (I mean "monstrous" with love, of course).

I'm just about to go to work in the temple. Athena needs no introduction really, but in case you have been living in a cave (hey, do you know my family?) the main things you need to know about her are that she is a super-important goddess. She is the goddess of WAR and WISDOM, which makes her quite a badass.

Athena lives on Mount Olympus with all the other Olympian gods. You know: Zeus, Poseidon, Aphrodite, Artemis, Demeter and so on - a whole complicated family tree

MOUNT OLYMPUS

ATHENA

HOME OF THE OLYMPIAN GODS

of **TWELVE IMMORTALS** who spend most of their time plotting against each other. The annoying thing is that we humans rely on these gods for **EVERYTHING**. It really gets on my nerves sometimes.

Need decent food to eat? Pray to Demeter.

Have to travel somewhere by boat? Better not annoy Poseidon.

Hoping to fall in love? Make sure Aphrodite is happy with you!

Humans aren't allowed to go up Mount Olympus, of course, but here, at the base of the mountain, every god has their own temple. On the whole the gods completely ignore us and go about their business as if we are nothing more than ants, but some humans are chosen to work for the gods in their temples. I hear the humans in Zeus's temple get to guard actual thunderbolts!

Supposedly, I should consider myself lucky to work for Athena. At least I'm not stuck working for sly, stinky Hades, god of the underworld – no human wants that! Hades isn't even liked by any of the gods either. Just the other day, Zeus sent out a message to everyone saying, ⟶

I mean, duh! Everyone knew that already. Hades isn't even an Olympian, yet he's just plonked a new well in the temple complex and it's already causing all kinds of problems. As I'm writing this, Athena and Aphrodite keep bickering about who gets to decorate the well. **WHO CARES? DOES IT REALLY MATTER? URGH.**

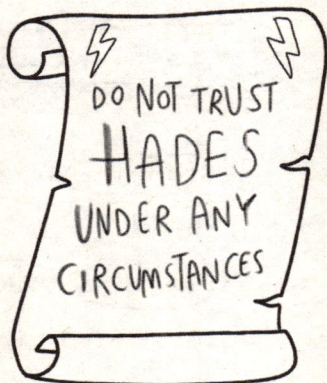

DO NOT TRUST HADES UNDER ANY CIRCUMSTANCES

5

As a guardian, I work and live in Athena's temple. Working for Athena is OK, I guess. Not boasting or anything, but I am the guardian of Athena's shield, which is by far her most **PRECIOUS** and **TREASURED** possession. There are other guardians, but I don't really talk to them much...

╔══════════════════╗
║ **MY JOBS INCLUDE:** ║
╚══════════════════╝

- (Standing) around in front of Athena's shield
- (Standing) around in front of an empty space where the shield should be, when Athena is out using the shield
- Cleaning the shield when Athena returns it, then ... you've guessed it ... (standing) in front of it again!

6

You may be wondering why a puny twelve-year-old human girl is guarding the prized possession of an all-powerful goddess. The gods can vaporize anyone with a click of their fingers, so it's a valid point. Why am I here? If anyone actually tried to take the shield off me, I'm not sure what I could do to stop them. Give them an icy stare, perhaps? I've had the same job for the last three years. And during that time a grand total of **NO PEOPLE** have attempted to steal the shield because, let's face it, Athena as goddess of war and wisdom is pretty much as all-powerful as you can get. You definitely don't want her as your enemy.

My best friend, Arachne, works for Aphrodite, the goddess of love. I wish we worked together, but it's the gods who choose. Arachne tells me that working in Aphrodite's temple involves singing beautiful songs while frolicking in sea foam, surrounded by tinkling shells, twittering doves and dancing dolphins. I really try hard not to be jealous but COME ON! My shield-guarding job is super boring, but I suppose it could have been worse (see: living in a cave).

There is one good thing about working for Athena, though: as the goddess of wisdom, she actually cares about her guardians' education – she wants to make us wise, so she has taught us to read and write. I am grateful for that. And it means I can write this diary! So, all in all, I'm pretty lucky, aren't I?

Human? ✓

Good job? ✓

Learning new skills? ✓

Awesome hair? ✓✓

Be honest, if anyone is actually reading this diary (although you shouldn't be, as it is my own private writings and therefore you should forever be cursed with bottom boils), wouldn't you want to be me? Wouldn't you want to be **MEDUSA GORGON?**

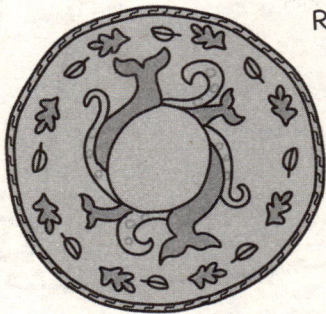

Right, now I need to go to work for another day of guarding Athena's shield. **Laters!**

HERMES EXPRESS
AIR TORTOISE (H.E.A.T.)

OFFICIAL CORRESPONDENCE BETWEEN
HADES AND ATHENA

Dear Hades,

I think there has been some mistake. You told me that I could decorate your new well, but Aphrodite thinks she is decorating it. Who is doing this? Please clarify.

Yours,
Athena

My dearest and most deliciously fiery-tempered Athena!

It is just SO EASY to wind you up! Chaos sown. Boredom alleviated. Another successful day for

HADES, god of the underworld

DAY ALPHA

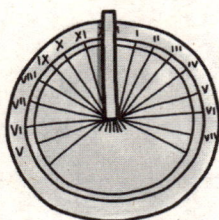

ATHENA'S TEMPLE, GUARDING SHIELD

Fine. OK, so the whole writing-a-diary plan will only work if I'm completely honest and, reading back my tablet from this morning, I maybe, perhaps, omitted certain facts.

The truth is I'm reeling from something my fellow guardians told me yesterday. They told me that they voted me **"the guardian most** likely to lose it and punch a god in the face"!

This is not good news.

In other words, they think I've got anger issues. **Charming, right?**

The other guardians in Athena's temple don't like me. When I first started, I tried to hang out with them all but I find big groups hard to deal with. You have to have the same opinions as everyone else and pretend to be everyone's best friend, even though actually everyone is really plotting against each other. Early on, I dared to mention that I found Athena a little ... scary ... and they all acted like I'd said the most shocking thing EVER. Having one good friend is so much better than being in a group like that!

I've learnt to keep my opinions to myself. I try hard every single day to make sure no one knows exactly what I think of the petty gods, my empty-headed fellow guardians and the ridiculous rules we all have to live by. It's not easy, as I'm with the guardians day and night. We don't really leave the temple that much, even when we're not officially working.

Apparently, the other guardians believe I am "tightly wound" – whatever that means. They think that one day, I'm going to go full monster on them and we'll all get punished. Ha! That's nonsense. They're probably just jealous of my poker face and voluptuous hair. The guardians have been listening to Cassandra too much; she works as an ORACLE in the temples around here. I really don't know why anyone still asks for her predictions about their future – she's a big old liar. She once told me that I would be famous throughout history for my terrible hair! As if! We all know it's totally glorious. She did also predict that Arachne would be one of the most famous

NONSENSE AND LIES

Blah blah, terrible hair, blahhhh...

weavers of all time – which I could totally see
– so maybe Cassandra doesn't lie all the time!

But, back to my so-called "anger issues". I'm
sorry to say the guardians are probably **RIGHT**.
But I have good reasons to be angry: I don't like
what I see the gods doing to humans (or, for
that matter, beasts, other gods and anyone or
anything else that displeases them). It makes
me **ANGRY**. They just give out punishments
when they feel like it and **IT IS NOT FAIR.**

This is serious stuff. In my world, a mistaken look can get you ripped to shreds (RIP Actaeon)! Can you see why I might be a teensy bit worried about my anger? If I can't control it, then I could land myself in real trouble. When I heard about what Artemis did to poor Actaeon, I really wanted to find Artemis and — well, that's the problem. What would I have done to the goddess of hunting if I'd found her? Had a stern word? Frowned? What can us humans do about any of it?

Absolutely nothing.

Zero.

ZILCH.

Do you know what it's like to feel completely and utterly powerless? To have someone in charge who lacks any kind of empathy or compassion?

What would **YOU** do about it?

YUP, that's right.

Also nothing.

Because we are human and they are gods.

I can't help my feelings, though. When things are unfair, it bothers me. And if I start feeling cross, my scalp tingles, my hair stands on end and I feel a hissing surging through my entire body. Sure, I've learnt to push those feelings deep down in my belly, but will they stay hidden forever? Finding out what my fellow guardians think of me maybe shows I'm not doing such a good job of masking my feelings as I thought.

But this is where Arachne's excellent gift comes into it. She's the only person worth anything around here, and she knows how I truly feel. She thinks that if I have an outlet for processing my feelings I might not be in danger of, well, **EXPLODING**.

And what is the outlet for processing my feelings?

Something that helps get those feelings out in a non-violent way?

It is...

Wait for it...

It ... is... Drum roll please...

WRITING!

Simple as that – writing.

Writing a diary about how I'm feeling will help get those feelings out! It's like a superpower. Instead of punching a god in the face, I can write down everything I want to say here, like:

YOU ARE A JEALOUS AND PETTY INDIVIDUAL AND DESERVE TO BE PUNCHED IN THE FACE.*

Or...

MAY ZEUS PELT YOU WITH THUNDERBOLTS AND POSEIDON PROD YOU WITH HIS TRIDENT FOR THE REST OF ALL TIME.

Or I can just scribble out a primal scream:

*I seem to have got a bit obsessed with punching in the face. Sorry about that. Don't punch people in the face, my boily-bottomed reader, whatever they have done.

And, miraculously, some of the anger leaves me. Everyone should try this – it's a lifesaver! Quite literally. For me, writing this diary could help save me from a fate worse than death.

I'm so lucky to have a friend like Arachne. She understands me. She's really chilled – and super creative. She deals with life by focusing on her weaving and embroidery. She should really be working for Athena, who is not only the goddess of war and wisdom but also handicrafts! **(Way to multitask. Who expected those skill sets to go together?)** I've been encouraging Arachne to show Athena her work, but she's really self-conscious about it. That's nonsense. I'd be proud to have her skills. I have **NO TALENT** for that kind of creativity. We've tried to teach each other our skills, and Arachne is doing quite well with learning her letters, but my ability to sew remains at zero.

But I want to do more for Arachne after her kind gift to me. I'll be thinking what I can do for her in return.

PARADOS

Shuffle up. Shuffle up. What have I missed?

What's going on?

Don't you know? This is a GREEK TRAGEDY!

And a Greek tragedy is...?

Oh, I despair! Didn't you read my notes? It was all on there. A Greek tragedy is "a drama that depicts the downfall of a basically good person".

So? What's that to do with us? Why are we all here?

We're the CHORUS! Every Greek tragedy has to have one.

But this isn't a play! Where is the theatre? Where is the audience?

As far as I can tell, we're just reading some poor girl's diary!

Yes, but it's a TRAGIC diary.

Doesn't seem that tragic so far.

Speak for yourself. I'm concerned about the bottom boils.

Well, in this story, as in any Greek tragedy, we have to meet the main character...

Medusa, right?

Well done. Yes, you've been paying attention. Then we have to learn what the story is about, and watch as the story unfolds.

That's all? We just read this girl's diary? I'm not sure there'll be much of a story.

You'll see. We have met our tragic heroine and —

She seems fine to me.

ACT I

DAY BETA

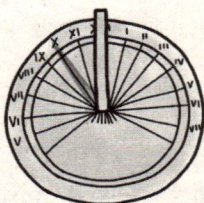

ATHENA'S TEMPLE, GUARDING EMPTY SPACE

Well, I thought I'd made a great start to my diary yesterday and was feeling lovely and calm after doing all that writing – but today I don't have very much to report. Athena turned up to take her shield out, so I have been left with very little to do. I wish more things happened to me – then I'd have more to write about!

I spent some of the morning wondering if there could be a better way of naming the days. I have started with α, then β, but what happens when I get through all twenty-four letters of the alphabet? Do I start again? What would those twenty-four days be known as? I think there must be a better way of doing this. I also think that me thinking about this is a sign of **HOW VERY BORING** working at Athena's temple is!

To the **ANNOYANCE** of the other **strict-rule-following guardians,** I did sneak out of the temple to see Arachne. I nearly got caught by Athena, but she was busy arguing with Aphrodite and didn't notice me tiptoe past her. When will those two ever stop **SQUABBLING**? Thankfully, Athena was so busy being angry at Aphrodite that she didn't notice me skulking in the shadowy gaps between the temple's columns. And I don't think she noticed Hades either, who

was also hiding in the shadows. He grinned and
chortled as he observed the goddesses arguing.
I'm surprised Athena and Aphrodite didn't spot
him – he's always accompanied by the whiff of
rotten eggs. **YUCK**.

Once I was out of the gods sight, I found Arachne.
You see, I have a great idea: if Arachne won't show her
amazing embroidery work to Athena, then I **WILL**. It
will be my gift to my friend, as thanks for this diary.
While Arachne was distracted by a low-flying baby

playing a harp (it happens quite a lot in Aphrodite's temple) I quickly grabbed her most recently finished embroidery. Once Athena has cooled down from her argument with Aphrodite, I'll show her my friend's awesome talent. But **DEFINITELY** once she's cooled down. I have learnt never to approach Athena when she's angry!

HERMES EXPRESS
AIR TORTOISE (H.E.A.T.)
OFFICIAL CORRESPONDENCE BETWEEN
HADES AND ATHENA

Dear Hades,

Is this really what you spend your time doing? Really? You have nothing better to do with your time than cause arguments? Daddy was right to warn us all not to trust you. But I do so wish to make the well look as good as I know it could. As goddess of handicrafts, I know how to make things look lovely.

Plus, if you let ME decorate the well, I'll help you learn how to spend your time more wisely. Maybe learn how to sew nice embroidery, rather than chaos? Wouldn't that be good?

Yours,

Athena

My dearest and most
admirably reasonable Athena,

Don't talk to me about your daddy. I know you
are entirely your own person and can make up
your own mind about everything. You don't need
old Sparky Beard giving you orders.

I do like how you, in your wisdom, are trying
to appeal to my reasonable side. How like
you, goddess of wisdom, to try to negotiate a
solution. "Oh, my name's Athena and I'm SO
WISE. Look at me dealing with epic battles
with intelligence and creativity. Aren't I
perfect? Worship me!" It must be lovely
being you.

Do you know what I get to deal with day
in, day out?

Dead people.

Awful, whiny, newly dead people, who all think
they deserve some special kind of treatment.
I get the good ones and I get the bad ones,
but I don't see any difference. They're all just
maggots to me!

"Oh, you've led a good life – here, spend the rest of time in the Elysian Fields,"
  or
"Oh, you've been very naughty – let me think up some evil punishment so you can be tortured for all time in Tartarus."

I've had an eternity of dealing with dead humans and I'm sick to the back teeth of it and of them. I'm SO BORED!

And then Zeus warns everyone not to trust me. How unfair is that? Am I not allowed to have a bit of fun? That's all I'm doing here. Having a bit of fun. Mr Big Boss, aka Zeus, aka your daddy, is just one massive party pooper. Ignore him! And, besides, it is SO EASY to wind you and Aphrodite up. Honestly, it's not even a challenge any more.

It's up to you and Aphrodite to sort out this problem.

Hades

P.S. In other words: LONG, WET RASPBERRY SOUND to you.

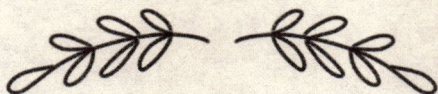

ATHENADAY (AKA DAY BETA)

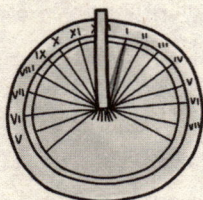

ATHENA'S TEMPLE, IN THE GUARDIANS' CHAMBER (FEELING NAUSEOUS)

What do you think of my new day-naming system? Good, yes? I can totally see it catching on.

Athena returned her shield after lunch. OK, so when I wrote that I wish I had more to do, **I DID NOT** mean that I wanted to spend most of this afternoon scrubbing off blood and disgusting bits of body goo from the shield. And I certainly did not want to find a bloody and squished eyeball in my hair later. Must have got there during the shield cleaning.

So, instead of showing Athena Arachne's work, I spent the rest of this afternoon vomiting, then heaving, and then washing my hair. I don't think it will ever feel clean again! My hair is ruined!

AAARRRRRGGGGGGHHHHHH.

KOMOS

Is it our turn? I think...

Nope. Not yet. Just keep reading.

APHRODITEDAY (AKA DAY GAMMA)

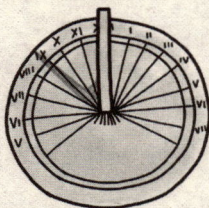

ATHENA'S TEMPLE, GUARDING SHIELD – AGAIN

Right. Today is the day.

IT

IS

HAPPENING.

When Athena calls by here this morning (as long as she looks fairly calm), I **WILL** show her

Arachne's beautiful embroidery. Maybe Athena will be so impressed, she'll ask Aphrodite for Arachne to come and work in her temple. We could become work besties as well as best friends. That would be so much better than working with these judgy guardians all the time. They've been giving me more weird looks than usual today. But anyway, I'm excited. I bet Athena will be majorly impressed with my super-talented friend.

APHRODITEDAY, LATER MORNING

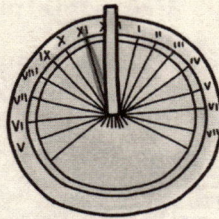

ATHENA'S TEMPLE, GUARDING SHIELD

It is done!

Athena swept haughtily into her temple just moments ago (to be fair, that is how she always moves. She's always haughty – it's not a reflection of her mood).

KOMOS

I quickly held out Arachne's embroidery, bowed my head and asked Athena (most graciously and as politely as I could muster) to admire my talented friend's work. Athena must have really liked the embroidery as she grabbed it and immediately asked about my friend. I told her that Arachne works in Aphrodite's temple, and off Athena swept.

I just wish I could have gone with her, rather than pointlessly staying around pointlessly guarding her utterly pointless shield (I mean, she is an immortal. What exactly is she shielding with it?) Instead, I find myself waiting. Fidgeting. I want to know what happened. I am only able to imagine how thrilled Arachne was to see Athena admiring her own handiwork.

The goddess looked like she couldn't believe a human could be so talented. Will Arachne come to work for Athena? Will we be work buddies?

Arachne looking thrilled!

This waiting is SO **FRUSTRATING!**

ATHENA'S TEMPLE, GUARDING SHIELD (STILL)

Why hasn't Arachne called by yet? Hopefully I'll catch up with her later. I did hear some yelling and a scream outside the temple a bit ago, but, to be fair, that's a common occurrence around here, so it's unlikely to have anything to do with my friend. She and Athena are probably holed up somewhere swapping embroidery and weaving tips.

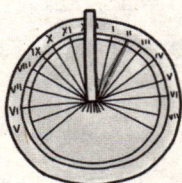

ATHENA'S TEMPLE, GUARDING SHIELD (WHILE PACING)

Come on, Arachne. Getting even more bored than usual, having to wait for you to turn up.

I keep listening out for footsteps, but I can see all the other guardians' eyes on me so I have to stay put.

I think I've just heard Aphrodite shouting at

someone outside. Aphrodite's voice is pure and clear – like the world's loveliest bell – even when she's angry. I wonder what's going on?

ATHENA'S TEMPLE, GUARDING SHIELD (WHILE PERCHED ON A LEDGE)

Just seen a weird creepy beastie with eight – EIGHT – legs and far too many eyes. Just had to write about it here.

YUCK.

Where is Arachne? I'd have thought she'd have visited me by now. She must know I want to hear how it went.

For now, I'm keeping my eyes on the beastie. I don't want it anywhere near me!

what is this WEIRD thing?

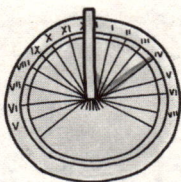

GUARDIANS' CHAMBER

Shift has ended and still no sign of Arachne.

Quite glad to be away from the shield, as that creepy-crawly thing kept appearing and trying to come towards me. I've never seen one before, but I don't like it.

Hopefully Arachne will turn up again tomorrow.

ZEUSDAY

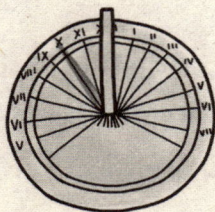

ATHENA'S TEMPLE, GUARDING SHIELD

The **WORST** thing has happened.

Is there a word that means **WORSE THAN WORST? MOST WORSTISOME?**

The **MOST WORSTISOME** thing has happened!

I arrived at work this morning, still concerned that I hadn't seen Arachne. THEN I noticed that creepy-crawly thing had returned to my area and spun some kind of silvery-thread-type thing that came out of its bottom! Totally disgusting. I didn't want to get close to it (it's really gross), but as I looked, I realized that the threads seemed to say something. They said:

ME IS ARACHNE!

Eh? NO! Surely I was imagining things. This horrible skittery beastie is my best friend?

I looked at EIGHT-LEGGED Arachne and asked what had happened. Had Athena not liked her embroidery? Creepy Arachne started to move again...

ATHENA JEALOUS- I NOW SPIDER

So that's what you call this type of creature – a **"SPIDER"**? I guess they're a thing now. The gods are always doing that – creating new things without telling us.

I don't want to be a weirdo whose best friend is a creepy spider (no offence, Arachne!). I thought Athena would love to see Arachne's craftwork. Arachne was her biggest fan, after all. How wrong was I? Athena's generally quite cool **(I mean, look at her, she totally rocks that helmet – who else could carry that off?).** ⟶

But woe betide anyone who gets on the wrong side of her. And turning my best friend into a spider? **OVER AN EMBROIDERY? WHAT IS WRONG WITH HER?** Yes, it is **THAT BAD.**

IT NOT THAT BAD

Athena has done this awful thing to Arachne OVER A PIECE OF SEWING, and there's nothing I can do about it. I can't think of a worse punishment. Being turned into a mega-creepy thing with eight legs is the most awful fate anyone could suffer – EVER. I think Arachne is incredible for trying to put a brave face on it (although, to be fair, I can't actually see her face, just a furry blob and quite a few eyes) but all I can do is just be a good little human and carry on like nothing has happened. I'm so angry.

In fact, writing this down is *not* helping my anger. Maybe some scream scribbling will help...

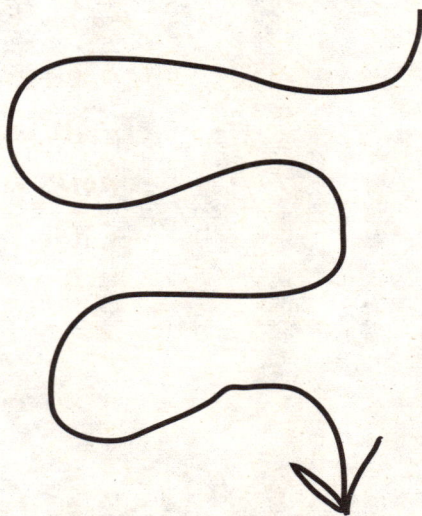

GRRRA
PPHHHR
HHH

AAAHHK

ROWWC

No. That's not helping at all. AND - worse still - I'm entirely to blame. I showed Athena her work. It's all **MY FAULT.** I'm going to have to do something - but what?

So what do you think so far?
I like the new names for the different days.
That's a very minor detail. What about the actual PROBLEM?
What problem?
Are you even paying attention back there? Medusa's best friend has been turned into a spider by Athena, and our protagonist blames herself.
That poor girl!
That poor spider!
I hate spiders – where's my hoover?
What's a hoover?
Things are definitely starting to go wrong, but is it tragic yet? I was promised tragedy.
WE WANT TRAGEDY
Let's see what happens next. Medusa is angry with Athena. How do you think that's going to go?

ZEUSDAY AFTERNOON

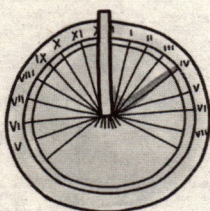

ATHENA'S TEMPLE, GUARDING SHIELD

I am still livid. I wish I could do something to help poor Arachne. I spent more time with spider-Arachne this afternoon. I'd like to say I'm not totally creeped out by her tiny hairy body and eight spindly legs. I'd like to say it, but, really, I **AM** totally creeped out. And I

tried to look her in the face, but when someone has **EIGHT EYES**, exactly which eyes do you look into? **It's creepy and confusing!**

Actually, Arachne seems pretty chilled with her new form. I allowed her to read my diary so far (OK, so random people aren't allowed to read it for fear of bottom boils, but my best friend can – also, not sure if spiders can get bottom boils?). She seems to want me to calm down about the whole her-being-turned-into-a-spider thing. She even listed all the reasons it's good to be a spider:

- No afraid gods
- Can go allwhere
- Can walk up walls and on seelings
- Delicious flies ← BARF
- Can still weave and sew – silks come out of my butt!

Hmmm, not sure I'll ever agree with Arachne on the positives of being a spider, but I'm pleased she is OK with what's happened to her. It doesn't make **me** any less angry, though. What Athena did to Arachne may go down in history as the worst punishment **EVER!** I can't imagine a worse fate.

Oh, and for the record, I will never - I repeat, **NEVER** - be on board with **butt weaving.**

KOMOS

ZEUSDAY

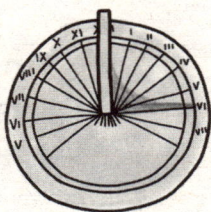

ATHENA'S TEMPLE, GUARDING
SHIELD (RESENTFULLY)

Nothing is helping. Every time I look at
Arachne, I'm overcome with anger towards
Athena. My best friend has been punished
in the most terrible way. Athena cannot be
allowed to get away with this. What can I do?
Writing **"I AM VERY ANGRY"** is simply not

going to deal with the magnitude of my rage.

What can I do against a god, though?

Me – a twelve-year-old girl, whose best (only) friend is a spider and whose job is to guard something that no one ever wants to steal?

Hang on.

I've got it!

I know exactly what I'm going to do!

HERMES EXPRESS
AIR TORTOISE (H.E.A.T.)
OFFICIAL CORRESPONDENCE BETWEEN
HADES AND ATHENA

My dearest and most soon-to-be-irate Athena,

Tee-hee-hee!

Hades

What now, Hades? I'm far too busy and important to deal with your childish messages.

A

Oh, you'll see, my dearest Athena. **You'll see.** Just a new bit of delightfully unexpected chaos. But I didn't cause it.

Hades

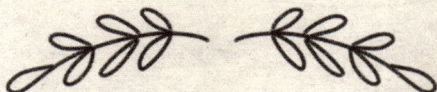

APOLLODAY

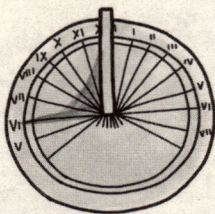

ATHENA'S TEMPLE, GUARDIANS' CHAMBER

Oh no, no, no, no. What have I done?

When I woke, I felt the sun on me – relaxing and soothing.

But then I opened my eyes and – HORROR!

Well, what I actually saw was

GOOD MORNING

This in itself was not the horror - it was remembering that my friend has been **TURNED INTO A SPIDER**

AND

also remembering that, in a fit of anger, with no other way to get back at Athena I ...

perhaps ...

may ...

have ...

possibly ...

thrown ...

Athena's ...

shield ...

into ...

Hades' well.

Oh my gods.

I think I'm going to be sick.

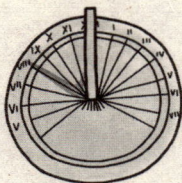

ATHENA'S TEMPLE,
GUARDING ... NOTHING

Still feeling sick. I just have to look at the empty space where the shield should be and waves of nausea flood through me.

I also feel sick whenever I see Arachne. That might be guilt, or it might just be that she now looks really gross (no offence, Arachne).

Can I get the shield back?

Could I jump into Hades' well after it?

To be fair, when I dropped it into the well yesterday (which, I have to admit, felt REALLY SATISFYING), I never heard it hit the ground or any water or anything. What exactly is down that well?

I'm surely not going to survive whatever

punishment Athena decides for me. I've shown my anger and done something terrible. Athena isn't exactly known for being reasonable.

Let's review:

- Creating a beautiful embroidery = PUNISHABLE BY BEING TURNED INTO A SPIDER
- Throwing away most prized possession = PUNISHABLE BY ?????????????

And yet ... actually, aside from the feelings of horror and the waves of nausea, there is something else I'm feeling today. I can sense it in the way I'm holding my chin just that little bit higher than normal. I can sense it in the smirk I'm giving my horrified fellow guardians. I can sense it in the burning in my chest. I think ... it's pride? It's being proud of finally standing up to a god – and it is my body's way of saying **"Ha! I'm NOT sorry"**.

Although I'm sure Athena will make me feel **VERY SORRY** – and soon. Athena will be on the warpath, and if there is someone you never want on a warpath, it is the goddess of war.

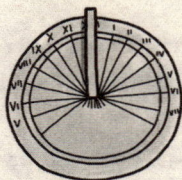

ATHENA'S TEMPLE, GUARDIANS' CHAMBER (HIDING)

Oh no, no, no, no, no, no.
I CAN'T EVEN...
I don't know how to begin.
Can I even bring myself to write about what has **JUST** happened?

Maybe I need to start by stating the worst part. And it is the worst. It is even more **worstisome** than Arachne's horrendous situation (no offence, Arachne).

Long story short:

ATHENA HAS CHANGED MY HAIR INTO SNAKES.

VILE, UGLY, ANGRY, SLITHERING SNAKES who won't stop hissing on top of my head.

I'm just going to let that sink in...

There. I've got the worst, most traumatic bit out.

I mean, I knew it was going to be bad. Let me tell you how it happened.

This morning I decided it was best to wait for Athena by the well, so I could tell her what I'd done, and hopefully explain that I had been very upset because I didn't think Arachne deserved to be turned into a spider. I had a speech all prepared.

When Athena arrived at the temple entrance, she completely blanked me as usual, so I called out,

"Athena! I was very angry that you turned my friend into a spider, so I have thrown your shield into Hades' well."

It was short and to the point.

Athena stopped in her tracks and turned to me.

Bum.

By now, a crowd of guardians from all the temples in the complex had gathered. I didn't want to look weak in front of them. I deserved punishment, but I wasn't going to apologize. Looking back, I'm not sure what I could've done to make my situation any better. But I probably didn't help matters by coming out with a speech that included the phrases **"stick it"**, **"piece of excrement"** and something about **"a bucket full of cold vomit"**. At least I didn't punch her in the face **Cha,**

shows what you know, fellow guardians!).

Athena glared at me for a moment and then raised her hand. Her invisible touch reached out, and my first reaction was to laugh, because my head began to tickle like mad. I put my hand up to scratch my scalp, only to feel something scaly – **WHAT WAS THAT?**

Thankfully, my question was answered rapidly, as someone from the crowd helpfully shouted out, **"Ewww – her hair is turning into snakes!"** Soon everyone was pointing and jeering at

what had appeared on my head.

I couldn't see the snakes, but I could feel thick, dry, scaly coils of serpents covering my head. I no longer had my lovely, luscious curls. My beautiful hair – gone! My eyes blurred as tears welled up and I opened my mouth to scream. The hissing around my head was unbearable. One of the snakes slid down my head to look at me and wink. **The cheek!**

"Anger me, girl, and this is what you get. Now everyone will see you for the forked-tongued monster that you are!" Then Athena laughed. She actually laughed!

As you can tell from my snake hair and spider-Arachne, Athena is nothing if not creative with her punishments. I guess being goddess of handicrafts DOES have its uses. Then I realized that this punishment, this head of snakes, was the worst that Athena could do to me. But I had survived it. I did not want her to see me upset. I fought my anger and the desperate feeling of unfairness. Then I turned and looked her straight in the eye.

This enraged her even more.

Athena raised both arms above her head, her face contorted in terrifying rage, and I stood firm, waiting for the worst. For the end. The crowd gasped, then collectively held its breath.

And **THEN**, before anything else could happen, there came the overpowering smell of rotten eggs. Hades! With a swish of black smoke he appeared next to Athena.

"Oh dear, Athena. Looks like you're having a bad day. Really channelling some top-grade fury right there."

"Shut up, Hades," snapped Athena. "Can't you see I'm busy?"

"Yes, true. You are definitely super busy and far be it from me to tell you how to punish any human. I must say, I'm loving the snake hair – you know I always admire your work, and, honestly, these foolish humans deserve torturing from here to eternity — but may I suggest that your planned punishment of this particular human wouldn't be the most ... effective use of her that's possible?"

"Oh, stop speaking in riddles and just spit it out, Hades." Athena was clearly keen to get on with punishing me, and did not appreciate Hades' interruption.

"Well, this unfortunate human has thrown your shield into MY well. I can't just let anyone into MY well. YOU can't go in there. But you can grant permission for someone else to go. Like this unfortunate girl here. I could send Medusa into the well, if you agree. Just imagine how dreadful this experience could be for her. Shield back for you, punishment for her, chaos and entertainment for me. Everyone wins!"

Hades sounded pretty proud of his suggestion,

and Athena appeared to be considering it. But me being sent down his well? That didn't sound any better than whatever Athena was going to do to me right then and there. What was that about everyone winning? Punishment for me was **not** winning. I figured I was already in enough trouble. What else could I lose? Why should the gods get to decide my fate?

"What if I refuse to go and get it?" I said.

"Oh, I like you!" Hades said. "You're showing some spirit. Good for you. But there must be something you want. Something that Athena can grant you if you get her shield back? How about you get your hair back? Or what about your spidery friend? Get back Athena's shield and Arachne could be returned to human form? Now you're interested, aren't you?"

He had a point there. This sly, untrustworthy (and really very stinky) god had suddenly become my one chance of saving myself and my friend. If there was a chance I could save Arachne, then I had to play along.

The crowd was getting bored now – they almost seemed disappointed that there wasn't going to be more drama. It was all just another day living among the gods for them. They started to drift away.

Hades grinned, linked his arm through Athena's and said, **"Come on, let's make a plan of the worst possible punishment for this human the world has ever seen."**

And, with that, they both walked off, leaving me in a fog of rotten-egg smell, alone by Hades' well. No, not quite alone. I had dozens of snakes hissing around my head.

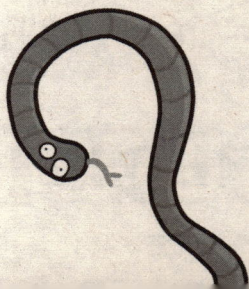

APOLLODAY

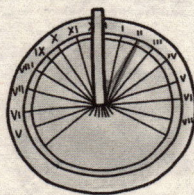

IN DEEP TROUBLE (AKA ATHENA'S TEMPLE - FOR NOW)

So much has happened today that my mind feels like it's about to explode. Just to be clear, that's nothing to do with the snakes on my head. I don't **THINK** they can do that. While I've been waiting for Hades and Athena to get back to me about their plan to send me through the well, I've been getting acquainted with my new **"friends"**. And, no, the guardians haven't decided that they like me. I'm referring to the slithering snakes **ON MY HEAD**. Can the punishment be worse than these serpents? (I'm not enjoying Apolloday – I hope it never catches on.) I've worked out that if I stay calm, they tend to stay relaxed too. But if I start thinking about how **MEAN** Athena is, I get angry and then they begin hissing.

If there is a chance I can save Arachne and get her turned back to being a human, I have to go for it. But if I've got this straight, I only have a chance of saving Arachne (and of getting my hair back) if I retrieve Athena's shield from Hades' well of doom. **Oh no!**

It's not like I can even turn to Arachne for comfort. She weaved the message:

THANKS TRYING STAND UP FOR ME

in her web, but that doesn't stop me from feeling awful – after all, she wouldn't be in this mess in the first place if it wasn't for me. I would have loved to give my best friend a hug but, honestly, I still find the spideryness quite off-putting. And, besides, I can't trust my new snakes not to EAT her. And that would be a really terrible way to end this already most terrible of days.

I have been doing some research and I think that what has happened to Medusa is more a case of HAMARTIA than hubris.
What?
You said that Medusa trying to stand up to Athena was HUBRIS. I think it's actually HAMARTIA. Hamartia is a flaw or error of judgement that leads the main character to place themselves equal to the gods. Isn't that what Medusa just did?
Erm, maybe.
And then what about anagnorisis?
Anagnor-what-je-me-flip?
Anagnorisis. It's when the main character realizes the web of fate they're entangled in.
That's just what's happened to Medusa! She now knows she's in deep doo-doo.
Doo-doo, diddy, did—
STOP THAT. And don't you be getting all technical with your language. We're not here for a Greek lesson. Just a good story.
You started it with your whole loo-brush thing.
Hubris!
See?

HERMES EXPRESS
AIR TORTOISE (H.E.A.T.)
OFFICIAL CORRESPONDENCE BETWEEN
HADES AND ATHENA

Hades,

OK, then. Let me hear your plan for punishing Medusa and retrieving my shield. Where exactly does your well lead?

Athena

My dearest and most eminently sensible Athena,

That's the beauty of my well. It is a portal to all space and time. Of course I am god of the underworld, so I've got the Elysian Fields, the Asphodel Fields and Tartarus all sorted. But, as death can strike anytime, anywhere, I need to be able to access all times and places too, and my well serves as a portal. With the well, I can go anywhere. It means I can also make your shield appear anywhere. Do we want Medusa trying to retrieve your shield from the Irish potato famine of 1845? Or maybe from the trenches in the First World War? During the Great Fire of London in 1666, perhaps? Or how about the epic Robot Uprising of 2237?

Hades

H·E·A·T

Hades,

Any of those sound PERFECT.

Athena

H·E·A·T

My dearest and most wonderfully wise Athena,

You'd think, wouldn't you? But I have learnt something from witnessing these moronic mortals throughout history. Under great pressure, humans tend to be ... better. It is when they have fewer problems that they actually get more petty, irritated and angry.

If you want Medusa to be endlessly frustrated and annoyed — pushed to the point where her anger will cause her to fail — then I have the perfect time and place in mind. Trust me on this!

Hades

Hades,

I know never to trust you! In fact, Zeus has warned everyone not to trust you. So why should I trust you now? Why can't you just go into your portal and get it yourself? Why send this girl? What's in it for you? I don't buy this whole **"chaos and entertainment for me"** explanation. What are you after?

A

My dearest and most startlingly brilliant Athena,

I'm very fond of chaos and entertainment! This punishment for Medusa sounds like the most deliciously enjoyable thing we'll have done in years. But I should have known I couldn't trick you.

OK. You got me. Don't spread this around as I do have my own reputation to think of – I don't want others knowing that I actually care what old Flashy Pants thinks. Zeus is barely talking to me. He wants me just to stay in the underworld forever and is hardly letting me do anything. In all honesty, I'm hoping that if I help you with this, you might put in a good word for me with him. You are his favourite daughter, after all.

And really, you don't have to properly trust me. We can set some ground rules. Tell you what, I'll draw up a contract. You can check it, sign it and everyone will be happy – yes?

Hades

MEDUSA PUNISHMENT CONTRACT

annotated by Athena

Between Hades, god of the underworld,

AND

Athena, goddess of war, wisdom and handicrafts

As part of the ongoing punishment of the mortal known as Medusa Gorgon, she has been tasked with retrieving Athena's shield from Hades' well.

Athena, goddess of war, wisdom and handicrafts, does hereby allow Hades, god of the underworld, to grant permission for the mortal known as Medusa Gorgon to be given access to his well and to be transported to a time and place of his choosing for the duration of this punishment. Should the mortal known as Medusa Gorgon succeed in retrieving the shield, Athena, goddess of war, wisdom and handicrafts, does hereby agree: to end all ~~future~~ current punishments* of Medusa ***not all future punishments. Athena reserves the right to punish her again in the future if the situation demands it.**

AND

to turn the mortal known as Arachne back to human form.

These humans will then remain in the employ of the gods Athena and Aphrodite.

The following rules have been agreed:

NUMBER ONE: Medusa can only travel back through the well when she has retrieved Athena's shield. She will not be able to return without it.

NUMBER TWO: While Medusa is in Hades' well, Hades will observe and report back to Athena. Hades himself can only enter the portal on the final day of the punishment. Athena will not interfere in Medusa's punishment. **Athena can request changes to the punishment if the reports displease her.**

NUMBER THREE: The task to retrieve the shield must be completed in a timely manner. Medusa's permission to be in the well will last for ~~500 years.~~ ⟨24 days⟩ **Honestly, Hades. It's like you know nothing about mortals. 500 years is impossible. And I am impatient for all this to end. Twenty-four days is all I am willing to allow.**

NUMBER FOUR: For the duration of her time

in Hades' well, Medusa's new snake hair will be masked by Athena **but only so long as Medusa keeps her temper.**

NUMBER FIVE: Medusa's requirements for living in the well will be met: shelter, clothing and food. She will also be provided with a couple of carers. **But no one too helpful, and not anything too luxurious. She's supposed to be suffering!**

NUMBER SIX: She will need to be able to speak and understand the language — **fine.**

NUMBER SEVEN: No other humans or creatures from ancient Greece will be able to enter the twenty-first century..

NUMBER EIGHT: Ways for Medusa to fail in the mission include, but are not limited to:

- She runs out of time.
- She tells someone who she is.
- She doesn't keep her temper and breaks Athena's masking spell..

NUMBER NINE: If Medusa fails in this task, she will be immediately returned to Athena's temple at the base of Mount Olympus. Athena will be permitted to continue her planned punishment of Medusa and Arachne will remain a spider..

I've added another couple of important rules:

NUMBER TEN: If Medusa fails in the mission for whatever reason, Hades will return Athena's shield to her by entering the portal himself.

NUMBER ELEVEN: Athena now has full permission to decorate the entrance to Hades' well in the temple complex at the bottom of Mount Olympus, and Hades has to tell Aphrodite she's not having anything to do with it. Ha!

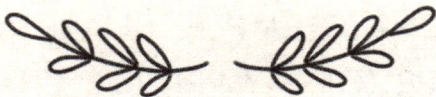

SIGNED:

HADES ___ *Hades* _____

ATHENA ___ *Athena* _____

MEDUSA ___ *Medusa* _____

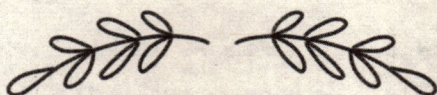

APOLLODAY

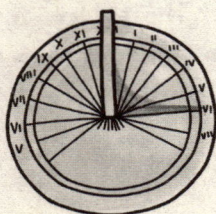

ATHENA'S TEMPLE, GUARDIANS'
CHAMBER (OR MY PRIVATE CHAMBER,
AS IT HAS BECOME!)

Tomorrow morning has been set as the time I will be sent into Hades' **WELL OF DOOOOOOOOOM.** Dread is seeping out of me as a cold sweat, just waiting for this fateful challenge to start. For now, I am staying in my chamber, away from all the gawping. Each time someone laughs or smirks at my new hair, humiliation and anger boil in my blood and, to make things worse, the vile snakes on my head respond by moving frantically. The angrier I get, the faster they move. Unfortunately, this was quickly realized by my fellow guardians **(and they told everyone – thanks a lot)** and so anyone who sees me now tries to anger me on purpose. I wish I could stop it. I wish I could cut them down with just one stare. That would show them. The good news, at least, is that my fellow guardians have had the sense to realize they don't really want to be hanging around when I've got a head full of angry snakes, so I'm alone in our chamber. So here I am, locked away and writing in my diary, hoping to calm the snakes.

Hiding away from everyone also gives me time to consider what I have got myself into. I definitely can't stay here and be punished

by Athena for all time, so I have to go along with this plan – it's my only chance of helping Arachne and the only way for me to get my hair back. Who would have thought Hades would be my saviour in this situation? I really don't think I can trust him, though. He called by earlier to give me my contract and he suggested I shouldn't tell people my real name when I'm through the well. He suggested using the name **"Meddy"**, as apparently the name **"Medusa"** is quite well known. Surely he doesn't mean that *I* am well known in this entirely different time and place to which I'm being sent? Why on earth should an unimportant human from ancient Greece, albeit one usually with great hair, be known? Hades didn't answer that, but he did take great pleasure in giving me more details about what I'll find in the well. Apparently the place I'm heading is full of godless humans, people who are selfish, tricksy and not to be trusted – a place with no discipline and no respect and where people worship only the soulless creations of man. It sounds truly awful. Unbelievably hideous. A place to strike fear into even the bravest heart!

And what is the name of this place, so reviled by the god of the underworld himself? Hades calls it **"a twenty-first-century English secondary school"**.

END OF ACT I

That's the end of the first act.
What? It was just getting interesting!
Well, we need to prepare for the change of scene. If this was an actual play—
Which it's not.
But if it was, the scenery on stage would need to be changed over and it gives the audience a break so they can mentally prepare for the story to change location.
Oh, goody. Does that mean I have time for a wee?
But we should be discussing what we've read. Analyse the action. Dissect the characters' motivations. Say what we think about THIS situation!
I think I need a wee.
Ugh. Go on then.
Excuse me. I've been reading up on this, and I think we've just witnessed the PERIPETEIA part of the story.
The what?
Peripeteia. Medusa's situation has changed from secure, as trusted guardian of Athena's shield, to vulnerable, with Medusa now being punished and sent on this quest. Isn't that Perip—
Oh yes, that. Of course I know about that. Parpytoes. Yes, exactly. I knew that. Oh, look. Is that t time? We need to get on with Act 2.
But Jeff isn't back from the toilet yet.

ACT 2

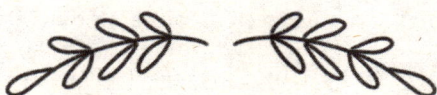

HƐRADAY

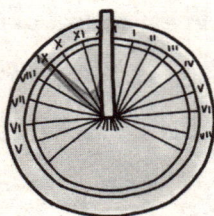

THE TWENTY-FIRST CENTURY.
SOMEWHERE COLD AND GREY

I barely know where to start with describing the last few hours. It has been **A LOT** to take in.

I was worried about the actual well itself, but after Hades **pushed** me into it as soon as the sun started to rise today (which he did with far more relish than was necessary), climbing out on the other side showed that the well itself was really the least of my worries. The place I've been sent to is completely unlike anything I've experienced. To be fair, I've only experienced the base of Mount Olympus and the cave where I was born, but even so ... everything here is just so ... **different**. Just how am I supposed to fit in here?

Before I left, Athena placed a spell over my head to cover the snakes, but even with the snake hair masked, **I CAN STILL FEEL THEM.** I knew the gods wouldn't play fair. It means I still need to concentrate on keeping calm, thinking gentle thoughts: blue skies, waves lapping the shore, birds twittering, etc. I feel like I stand out too much, even though I'm wearing clothes that are supposed to help me fit in to this new time. These clothes feel strange and uncomfortable. My lower half

is covered in something called **"jeans"**, which are apparently a kind of "trouser". On my top half, I'm wearing a **"T-shirt"** in a weird, stretchy material. The only stretchy material I knew in ancient Greece was pigs' bladders. Please tell me I'm not wearing something made from a **pig's bladder!** What was wrong with a light cotton chiton or a woollen peplos? I fear my new, ridiculous outfit is part of Hades' punishment, or, perhaps, a cruel joke. At least we are all dressed the same. And when I say **"we"**, I'm talking about me and my so-called **"carers"**.

The gods have decided that the best **"carers"** for me are my sisters

Stheno

and

Euryale.

STHENO

EURYALE

OK, so they're a few years older than me, but they're also two sea monsters who have lived in a cave all their lives. My sisters are less use than a broken urn! I knew the gods would do something like this. At least they've given Stheno and Euryale human bodies for the duration of my mission – but I can't see how they are going to be remotely helpful, when they're only just learning how to walk, and breathe through their noses. OK, got to stop complaining about that now, as it's only making me more annoyed. I can feel the snakes moving about on my head as my anger increases.

And breathe...

I'm fine.

I'M FINE.

The gods want me to lose my temper, but if I keep breathing, telling myself I'm fine and writing in this diary, hopefully I'm in with a chance of keeping control – aren't I?!

Anyway, the exit of the well turned out to be right in front of some metal railings that surrounded a large grey building with big columns. The building looked a bit like one of the temples from my time, just unloved and much scruffier. I could read the name above it:

SHADEWELL ACADEMY

The gods promised to help me understand the language – and it was working! So that is the secondary school where Athena's shield is kept in this particular time. It does, indeed, look like a frightful place. But it appeared to be quiet and empty. For a brief moment, I hoped the element of surprise meant I could just rush in there and complete my mission immediately. While Stheno and Euryale were still finding their balance on their new human legs, I ran to the gate and rattled it, determined to get in and find the shield. The sooner I can escape this strange place, the better. But of course Hades wasn't going to make my punishment that easy.

An old wrinkled woman with a bright-red sleeved cloak – probably a witch – passed me and said, **"Oh, it's so nice to see a child keen to go to school! But it's the week-end, love. Try again tomorrow!"**

What did she mean? Surely **EVERY** child knows how lucky they are to be given an education? I felt lucky to be taught reading and writing as part of working for Athena. But to be actually sent to school? And not just the boys? Shouldn't children at a secondary school be the happiest children ever?

(Note to self: find out what a "week-end" is. Is it good or bad?)

HERMES EXPRESS
AIR TORTOISE (H.E.A.T.)
OFFICIAL CORRESPONDENCE BETWEEN
HADES AND ATHENA

Hades,

So, I'm ready to hear about Medusa's suffering. When does her punishment start? Is she already howling with pain, Hades? Come on — you're supposed to be reporting all this to me! Tell me what's going on.

Athena

My dearest and most impatiently bloodthirsty Athena,

You need to have patience. Medusa will be thoroughly punished. And it will be BEAUTIFUL.

Hades

HERADAY

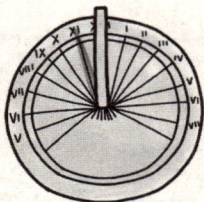

"HOME"

We have managed to make it to what will be our home for the twenty-four days (or, hopefully, just the next day or two). To be honest, I'm surprised we made it here in one piece, even though it's only on the other side of the square to the school.

I was worried that people might stop and

gawp at three bizarrely dressed girls suddenly appearing out of a well – no strangers could turn up in the temple complex without everyone noticing. But no one gave us a second glance. At first, I was relieved to see that our odd clothes were, actually, what most others were wearing too. Observing these twenty-first-century people, an uncomfortable feeling settled in my stomach as I noticed they all had their heads down, looking at small slim rectangular boxes in their hands. How strange. Are these people slaves to some kind of weird **RECTANGULAR OVERLORD**? Maybe that's why Hades was so keen for me to come to this place? Am I going to be ruled over by a small slim rectangle as well?

The more immediate danger on our short journey was something called **"CARS"**.

CAR = DANGEROUS

We nearly died several times. Note: look out for these and avoid them at all costs.

My sisters were particularly in danger of being squashed because they kept seeing their reflections. It turns out there are a lot of reflective surfaces in the twenty-first century. There's something called "glass", which is an amazing thing to stop window holes being just ... holes. It's probably a very good job they've got glass here, because it is **DEFINITELY** not as warm as Greece. People would freeze without glass in their windows. But each time Stheno and Euryale saw themselves in window glass, I had to spend another few minutes trying to get them to move along. It was almost as if seeing themselves in human form made them turn to stone! I didn't want to look in the windows too much. Even though the snakes aren't actually visible, the hissing in my ear is enough to remind me of what is on my head.

Things didn't get much better in our new house. We have lots of windows, which excited my sisters greatly, but they were even more fascinated to see a **twenty-first-century** mirror. To be fair, they are so much clearer than the highly polished brass mirrors from our time – but I think it takes more to impress me. My sisters were impressed by a simple door! **(You don't really get doors in caves.)**

The house is far smaller than Athena's temple, but if this is how normal humans live in the twenty-first century, perhaps it won't all be bad. There's no majestic marble columns or sweeping stone stairs, but the house is made up of several rooms, including a bedroom each – **what a treat!**

It took my sisters a while to understand that there is one room with facilities to make food and drink, and a totally different room for washing. The **"bathroom"** holds a private latrine that is quite marvellous – you can flush away the waste, and the seat is far more comfortable and warmer on the buttocks than the stone slabs in the temple. I did catch Euryale trying to drink from the **"toilet"**, so had to explain that we have a separate **"kitchen"** for those things – but I think I'll need to keep an eye on her, as she seemed to be really enjoying the toilet water. Looks like I might have to be the one "caring" for my sisters, not the other way round. **Oh dear.**

The kitchen contains a "hob", which gives us immediate fire – a miracle Prometheus would be proud of (if he wasn't busy having his liver ripped out as punishment from Zeus for giving humans fire in the first place). There's also something called a "fridge", which keeps things cold. I'm not sure it's needed in this very chilly place. Maybe my torture is simply going to be being frozen to death in this horribly cold place called "England".

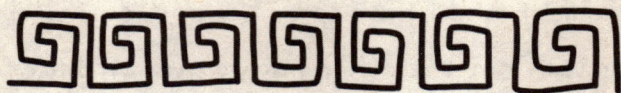

HERADAY –
SUNDAY 25 JUNE

MY NEW BEDROOM!

I have been learning a lot about this new time, even just in the last couple of hours since I wrote in my diary. For one thing, they have their own calendar, so I don't need to keep going with my own. Today is apparently "Sunday" here (although there is nothing sunny about it) and we are in something called the month of June.

I know these things because, to our great relief, we haven't been left entirely without assistance. Hades has granted us the services of:

AN ORACLE!

In the main room, which contains comfortable soft seats, floor coverings and magical lights that come on simply with the flick of a switch, there is a special cylinder.

This wondrous object is a direct way to communicate with the most divine **Oracle Alexa.** She must be a great and powerful oracle indeed. Perhaps she is so powerful that we humans are not allowed to look upon her directly, for fear of being

exploded into billions of pieces? Or perhaps she is shy? I cannot question the methods of this great oracle, but must show her the respect she is owed. I make sure I bow to her regularly.

Most of this afternoon has been spent preparing for me going to school tomorrow. Starting school? How hard can that be, right? I have been working for three years, so going to school should be a doddle, yes? The problem is, I'm not so sure. So far the twenty-first century doesn't seem as terrible as Hades described, so I assume this **"secondary school"** that I'm supposed to be going to will be an absolute nightmare. I can only imagine the monsters I'm about to be faced with.

KOMOS

The twenty-first-century secondary school sounds like it's going to be **APPALLING.**

OH NO. How can Medusa possibly survive this new horror?

NOW it's a tragedy.

Great, let's crack open the popcorn and see what Hades has in store.

Oi! Whose side are you on?

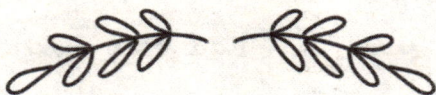

MONDAY 26 JUNE,

WHERE AM I? OH YES, A COMPLETELY NEW TIME AND PLACE

A bit of a rude awakening this morning. A loud incessant honking sound blared through the house at the time I needed to rise - apparently Stheno and Euryale had asked the Oracle Alexa to wake me at an appropriate time. Is that them acting as my carers? I suppose I should try to be grateful. I had been worried I was going to be late for school, as the weather is too grey for me to be able to read the sundial I'd set up. Maybe people in England don't pray to Helios enough – the god of the sun is clearly sulking and not doing his job of dragging the sun across the sky properly.

I'm surprised at how quickly my sisters have settled into our home. They have already got over their excitement at using a door and seeing lights come on as if by magic (which I'm still pretty awed by), but they've barely stopped gawping at themselves in the fancy shiny mirrors and are OBSESSED with their new looks. I should be pleased for them, but it's hardly fair that I have to go to school and complete my mission, while they, being eighteen, just get to hang around in our house. It is also mega unfair that I, Medusa of the notoriously amazing hair, have been cursed with snake hair that I have to try hard to keep under control, while my sisters have been granted completely new human forms. Gone are the scales and claws and really hideous faces **(and I mean REALLY hideous)**, to be replaced by pleasant features and hair that would rival mine even on a good day. I can't help but think that Athena did this just to annoy me. My hair, on the other hand, doesn't look **QUITE** so glorious as usual. The spell is working to disguise my snake hair, but I miss my luscious locks.

Maybe I should see my time here with my sisters as an opportunity to get to know them better. After all, it's been years since we shared a cave together, and I always felt kind of bad, because I look like this, while they ... don't. But Stheno and Euryale are basically ignoring me and are busy chatting away with the Oracle Alexa like she's their best friend. They don't seem to want to do anything else. Who knew that growing up in a dark cave would be the perfect preparation for life in the twenty-first century? I'm not sure they should bother the Oracle Alexa this much – she'll surely tire of answering their questions and might even get angry, like the gods at home. They have discovered that Oracle Alexa will provide things for them if they ask. This is quite amazing, but I am cautious. We don't want to take advantage of this powerful oracle. Having said that, I am running out of space on my wax tablets, so have requested a new tablet. I don't think Oracle Alexa minded.

But since Stheno and Euryale are busy with the Oracle Alexa, I'm stuck on my own, trying to sort myself out for school – or "SHADEWELL

ACADEMY", as it is known. I don't know why the gods granted me twenty-four days here. Surely I can just grab the shield as soon as I locate it and return through the portal? For that, I'll barely need one day! The key to success will be keeping calm (in other words: keeping my temper) and *NOT* doing anything that calls attention to me. Which also means dressing in Shadewell Academy's uniform, which is as dull and grey as the weather in this place. Being twelve, I have been able to dress myself for years, of course, but in this new time there are strange new ways to attach clothing and fix garments together. What was wrong with a simple pin or brooch? What, in the name of Zeus, is a "zip" or "Velcro"? Are those even words?

And don't get me started on this thing that I first thought was some kind of torture

device. It took me ten minutes to realize it didn't wrap round my head as a bandage for toothache! After an age, and at risk of being late for school – because **NO ONE WAS HELPING ME (Grrrrrrrrr. Thanks, diary – snakes are calm for now)** – I realized it was something to hold up my not-very-existent breasts. What has happened to women's breasts in this time that means they require such highly engineered clothing? The older guardians in the temple would wear their leather strophions for support – but these new **"bras"** are something else. It's very uncomfortable and the cups are all **flippy-flappy** under my shirt.

Before I left for school, Stheno **(who is apparently now an expert on doors)** told me to take a key with me, and to make sure I look after it. I have put it in one of the saggy bra flaps, so I guess my bra does have its uses after all!

SHADEWELL ACADEMY, GIRLS' TOILETS

Wow. Starting a new school is hard. I'm using all my energy trying to understand how things work here, so I'm now hiding in the toilets to write this, just to give me a break and help keep my snakes calm.

I am apparently a Year 7, which means that I am the least important kind of person here and I need to move out of the way of anyone bigger. That's nothing new. When you live among the gods, you quickly get used to being the least important person. I needn't have worried about trying not to call attention to myself. Even when I was ushered into a big room and introduced to all the children in there as **"Meddy Gordon"** (another thing I've got to get used to), only one child paid me any attention at all – a girl with a heavy fringe and big grin gave me a friendly wave. Everyone else was just looking down into their laps, playing with those small slim rectangles I'd seen people with yesterday. The teacher occasionally pleaded with them to put the rectangles away, but she was just ignored.

The teacher, who wore a dress of the most startling purple, introduced herself as my **"tutor and English teacher"**, Miss Morley, and the class as my tutor group **"7M"**, whatever that is, and part of **"Austen House"**, whatever *that* is. Miss Morley asked if I had any initial questions.

I said, **"Yes. What type of beetles were ground up to create the colour of your dress?"**

A brief cloud flashed over Miss Morley's face, and I realized that my question was probably considered very rude and disrespectful. I flinched, covering my head with my arms, waiting for punishment. My snakes quivered beneath Athena's masking spell.

"I'd have to check the label but I'm fairly certain it's a man-made dye," she said, looking confused.

Was that it? And what's a label?

Here was an adult in a position of authority over me. I had done the wrong thing and ... nothing. Just pleasantness! Even when Athena wasn't around, in Athena's temple, the female elders were in charge and woe betide anyone who was not at their post or being disrespectful. If Hades thinks this place will be a great punishment for me but adults here don't punish rudeness, something else must be going on. Maybe people here secretly eat children or something?

Miss Morley gave a nervous tinkling laugh and

continued, "I understand you've just arrived from somewhere ... else — I'm a bit unclear on that information as we don't yet have your transfer details. But I can assure you that we do not raise a hand to our pupils. It's a long time since corporal punishment has been used in schools here." Miss Morley paused, cleared her throat and gave me a look of — well, I'm not one hundred per cent sure what the look was, because I've never seen it from an adult, but I think it might have been sympathy. **"Let's get you shown around. Inna, would you like to...?"**

The smiley girl started to stand — for a moment, I was really pleased that she was going to show me around. She looked nice. But suddenly a girl in front of her jumped up instead. This other girl glared at Inna, scraped her chair back, placed her sparkly pink rectangle in her pocket and grumpily swished her long brown hair as she joined me at the front of the class.

"I'll take Meddy around, Miss. I know the school much better than Inna," this other girl said in a bored-sounding drawl.

I was hoping Miss Morley would insist on Inna giving me the tour, rather than this girl who kept rolling her eyes, but the teacher just sighed and said, "Fine, Sophie. Make sure Meddy knows where everything is. Show her the ropes."

Ropes? What ropes? Ropes that teachers tie bad children in? I started to worry that my worst fears about this place were true. And it wasn't helped when Sophie spoke again.

"Do I get to show her the dungeons, miss? Or the torture chamber?"

Ah! There we go. I took in a deep breath and I prepared myself for some truly gruesome sights, but Miss Morley just laughed, and in the end Sophie only showed me boring grey "CLASSROOMS" and where the toilets were (actually, the toilets are, to be fair, pretty gruesome). She pointed out the no-go areas of the staffroom, caretaker's cupboards and the basement, which is completely off-limits to pupils.

"Is that where the dungeons are?" I asked.

Sophie just rolled her eyes and carried on. She seemed determined to show me every last detail of the school. The tour lasted all morning, and Sophie chatted away to me as we walked around. We went outside to the "playground", where Sophie pointed out, just next to the exterior door, something called **"GUM MOUNTAIN"** (spoiler alert: it was a shiny grey mound, about as tall as my knee, that smelled vaguely minty. Mount Olympus it was not). At the far end of the playground Sophie gestured to some seating and said that was where all the "**cool**" kids hang out, and that I should join her there with her friends at break.

GUM MOUNTAIN

"**I'd much rather be somewhere warm, thank you very much,**" I said, which made Sophie laugh. I have no idea why.

No wonder kids are cool here. Compared to ancient Greece, England is absolutely **FREEZING!**

Supposedly, I can understand and speak the

language of the twenty-first century, so I can fit in here – but there's a big difference between **UNDERSTANDING** what people are saying and **ACTUALLY KNOWING WHAT THEY'RE TALKING ABOUT,** which is why I think Sophie found me strange company, to say the least. She asked me lots of questions,* but when I failed to answer a single one to her satisfaction, Sophie gave up trying to engage me in conversation. Instead, she got out her **"phone"** (so THAT'S what you call those small slim rectangles) and, magically, moving cats doing super-cute things appeared on it. She seemed to accept this as entirely normal, so I tried not to gasp in wonder as I watched the fluffy little marvels. Is this how the evil overlords get you? It was certainly hard not to fall into some kind of trance while watching the cats.

"I'll be in trouble if we get caught," she

said, "but everyone is in lessons, so we should be safe."

I asked if that was when she would be put in the dungeons she'd mentioned earlier, but she just giggled and then looked at me like I had three heads.

I don't get it. Sophie didn't seem at all bothered that she might be punished for doing

121

the wrong thing. What is so terrible about this place? What has Hades got in store for me?

I was glad when Sophie announced (actually, a very loud bell announced and Sophie explained) that it was lunchtime. Sophie said I could sit with her and her friends, who are all really **"lit"**.

I said, "Thanks, but I'm finding these electric lights are helping illuminate everything really clearly."

Sophie simply laughed again. I get the feeling I keep saying the wrong thing. I definitely said the wrong thing to the ladies who were serving lunch. Brown sludge in big trays was being dolloped on to smaller trays that the children were holding. It did **NOT** look appetizing. When it was my turn, I asked if they perhaps had some honey, olives or figs. I got a grunt in response. Giving up on decent food, I hoped that I could at least quench my thirst after my long tour, so I asked for some wine. This didn't go down well. What kind of place doesn't serve wine? The dinner lady asked for my name, saying she'd make a note on my record. Oh dear, that doesn't sound good.

As confusing as this morning has been, I can't forget why I'm here. I need to save Arachne, so I **must** find that shield, which means I'll have to leave the safety of these (really disgusting) toilets at some point and face the afternoon. I have learnt one useful thing – the shield is definitely not in these toilets!

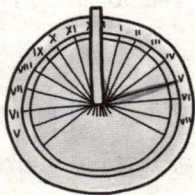

HOME, MY ROOM

It's safe to say that my first day at school could have gone better. I'm so pleased to be home,

even if my sisters – my so-called "carers" – are basically ignoring me in favour of the Oracle Alexa. At least here I can be more myself and not worry about doing or saying the wrong thing. And I have taken off the bra. I don't care if my breasts are in danger of dropping off. Nothing is worth the torture of a bra.

This afternoon, I had my first actual lesson at Shadewell Academy, which I was really excited about. I left the safety of the toilet after lunch, determined to make a good impression and not be considered a troublemaker (unlike at the temple). Until I can work out how to find the shield and get it back to the well, I have to fit in as much as possible. But that might be too much to ask if this first lesson was anything to go by. It started with the teacher, Mr Philson, asking me if I like science. I had no idea what "science" was (and I've since asked the Oracle Alexa how

to spell the word – if you'd given me a hundred guesses, I still don't think I'd have landed on **S-C-I-E-N-C-E!**). I looked at him blankly, until he said, **"You know – how we understand the world. How the world started – that kind of thing."**

Well, I know all about that! Athena made sure we knew how the world began while we were learning to read and write, so I started saying proudly, **"Yes, I know about Mother Earth – or Gaia, to give her correct name – emerging from Chaos, then creating her children: Uranus, the three Cyclopes and the Titans."**

Mr Philson stared at me for a second, took in a deep breath that caused one of his hairy nostrils to whistle, and then simply said, "You have a lot to learn."

"Yeah," a boy from the back of the classroom piped up. **"Like Uranus is actually a bum hole!"**

The whole class started laughing - in fact, Sophie clapped, did a flick of her hair and said, "Oh, Oscar, you're SO FUNNY!" - but I was just really confused. Not about the bum hole (although I'm not sure Uranus would be happy to have things like that said about him - he's not known for being able to take a joke) - but this teacher was telling me I was completely wrong. Have the gods been lying to me this whole time?

After a hard day, I was delighted to find that my new writing tablet had arrived when I got home. The Oracle Alexa is indeed great and powerful - but I think "tablet" means something else now. The new tablet was not made out of wood, which surprised me. I melted my wax and poured it on, hoping it would

be ready to use tomorrow - but **NOOOOOOO.**
Apparently you should not cover a twenty-first-century tablet in wax.

How was I supposed to know that?

Very kindly, the Oracle Alexa has ordered me another one. I am worried we are taking advantage of her too much. My sisters just completely monopolize her, asking for all kinds of things. But every time we ask her for something, this weird squiggly sign appears: (£)

Maybe it means **"questions answered"**, as there are numbers next to it that keep going up and up. I tried to spend some of this evening befriending the Oracle, so she knows she is appreciated. I had collected some flowers on the way home from school and draped them

£ BANK STATEMENT
YOU'VE SPENT £40
£100
£200

round her. I need her to like me. She's the key to learning more about the twenty-first century - and I need all the information I can get if I'm going to fit in here and succeed in my mission to get Athena's shield back and save Arachne.

HERMES EXPRESS
AIR TORTOISE (H.E.A.T.)
OFFICIAL CORRESPONDENCE BETWEEN
HADES AND ATHENA

H.E.A.T

Hades,

What am I waiting for? I should either be receiving my shield any time now, or Medusa should be failing and being tortured by her situation. Either way, I want to hear more about her misery.

A

H.E.A.T

My dearest and most delightfully demanding Athena,
Oh, the misery is coming. She is baffled and confused and disorientated. This is just the first stage. Hold on to your helmet, Athena — Medusa is in for a WORLD OF PAIN.

Hades

TUESDAY 27 JUNE

08:30

HOME, SITTING IN THE KITCHEN

I now have my new (new) tablet and my sisters have helped me set it up. It doesn't require any wax but I can write with a stylus *AND* it records it and I may never have to use a wax tablet ever again. How amazing is that? Now I can jot down all my thoughts and emotions and not worry about running out of space. If yesterday was anything to go by, this diary is the only thing that's going to help me survive here.

And I must control my emotions if I want to save Arachne. I HAVE to save her.

Speaking of emotions, I'm feeling even MORE NERVOUS about school today. I can feel the snakes being all jittery on my head (thankfully, under Athena's masking spell, of course). I am determined to make a better impression today. Last night, I asked the Oracle Alexa about how to fit in better at school, and she suggested some things to supposedly make me "popular", and she talked about **"loving myself"** and developing **"healthy self-esteem"**, which, not to be rude, all sounded like nonsense.

13:10

SHADEWELL ACADEMY, GIRLS' TOILETS (AGAIN)

Oh dear, I appear to be hiding in the toilets again

this lunchtime. I've learnt not to ask for wine (definitely don't try this at school – it angers the dinner ladies and resulted in a very serious meeting with Miss Morley, who lectured me on the dangers of underage drinking...) but I'm not sure I've made a better impression with Sophie and her friends.

When I arrived, I was pleased to see Inna, the friendly-looking girl from 7M. She seemed to be waiting in the entrance to say hello to me, but before she could open her mouth, Sophie swept up with her friends and gave Inna a fierce glare, like she had dared to use Sophie's brand-new comb. (I was the comb in this scenario.) This kind of glare was a regular occurrence between the guardians in Athena's temple. Sophie continued to glare at Inna, while dragging me to our first lesson.

"Avoid Inna," said Sophie. **"She's weird. If you want to be popular at school, don't go anywhere near her. You're best off sticking with me and my**

friends. No one would be seen dead with Inna. She's always reading books and I don't think she even has a phone. If she wasn't so, you know, weird, I'd almost feel sorry for her!"

That's exactly the kind of helpful insight I needed from the Oracle Alexa – not some guff about loving myself and self-esteem. Pah! Sticking with Sophie's group seems a much better approach. And Sophie and her friends all have great hair, so it feels only natural that I'd be friends with them.

In the history lesson, as our teacher, Mr Warburton, handed out lots of identical books, he asked me what history I knew, so I started talking about Cronos and the Titans and the fight with the Olympians (learnt through reading, thank you very much!). He interrupted me and said that I was, "Talking about ancient Greek mythology, not **actual** history, and you need to learn the difference between make-believe and reality."

Make-believe?

MAKE-BELIEVE?

I could feel the snakes responding as a mixture of anger and embarrassment twisted through my body. Not only had the teacher belittled me, but he had also cut me off mid-sentence. I wanted to fix the teacher with a glare so focused that it would pierce his skull – but instead I closed my eyes and tried to breathe deeply, repeating the words "I'm fine" in my mind. My anger subsided and I could feel the snakes settle back down.

That was a close one. I opened my eyes and looked around. No one seemed to have noticed

my hair doing anything strange. Mr Warburton had already moved on to asking questions to other pupils, about somewhere called "America". I buried my nose in the book the teacher had put in front of me and tried to focus.

At lunchtime, Sophie and her three friends (Olivia, Orla and Ottilie) asked me to sit with them, which was great – to begin with. I'd just grabbed my lunch from the dinner lady (who clearly remembered me from the whole "wine" incident) and sat down at their table, when Sophie started talking about the boys in our school. She asked me if any of them had caught my eye. Caught my eye? Yuck! I'm here to find the shield and save Arachne, not to lose my head over a boy. Not that I could say that. So I just mumbled that I'm not that interested in boys.

Ottilie said, "Well, if you change your mind,

stay away from Oscar. He's Sophie's crush."

Oscar? The boy with the bum hole? (You know what I mean.) Ugh. No way. Sophie is completely welcome to him or any of the boys here, thank you very much. I was just thinking about how completely uninterested I am in boys, when one of the girls – Olivia (probably) – said, "Oh my god, I love your hair," and put her hand out to touch it.

I panicked. I didn't know whether she was going to feel hair or lots of snakes. And would the snakes bite her? I had no idea. I did the only thing I could think of, which was shouting, **"Don't touch my hair!"**

Really loudly.

Thankfully, it did at least do the trick. Olivia retracted her hand faster than if she'd **actually** been bitten by a snake. And then there was silence. It was rather awkward. But

what else could I have done?

"Too right, Meddy. I don't like anyone touching my hair either. You tell her," said Sophie, coming to my aid.

And everyone laughed. But if you want to make friends with a group of girls, it's probably best not to start by shouting at one of them. The rest of lunch was uneasy to say the least, and they all seemed relieved when I said I was heading to the toilet, which is where I am now.

20:52

HOME

Well, I have to admit the Oracle Alexa must be pretty powerful. Everything Stheno and Euryale asked for yesterday has turned up, including a "phone" each. It turns out that, while I was trying to fit in at school, my sisters were learning all about the twenty-first century. We must be on some kind of record for the number of questions asked of the Oracle, as the number that flashes next to the "£" on my tablet is super high. But now my sisters have their phones, they are ignoring Oracle Alexa. This gave me my chance! I tried to quiz the Oracle about things I've been learning at school, in the hope it would help for my next lessons, but she was giving me the silent treatment. Perhaps she's sick of being endlessly asked for things. As a tribute, I laid the bones from our dinner around her cylindrical tube. Hopefully that will make her feel more appreciated.

KOMOS

WEDNESDAY 28 JUNE

08:09

HOME, KITCHEN

Turns out the Oracle Alexa had run out of power! My sisters worked out how to feed her, so Oracle Alexa is pleased and is talking to us again. What a relief! I don't understand how humans have captured this magic called electricity. It even powers their oracles these days! No wonder these people don't feel the need to pay attention to the gods any more, if they have powers like this! If Prometheus was punished simply for giving humans FIRE, who has been punished for these new developments? Whose liver is being ripped out on a daily basis in Tartarus for giving humans electricity?

How loud was the BIG BANG?

What is America?

Who gave humans ELECTRICITY?

13:08

THE TOILETS – AGAIN!

So I have **definitely** blown my chances of being

part of Sophie's group of friends. Do I feel sad about this? **Absolutely not!** I've changed time and place but not personality. I didn't like being part of a group in the temple, so why should I like being part of one here? And Sophie's group definitely reminds me of my fellow guardians; they're always judging everyone else, particularly me. This morning I was really trying hard to get back into their good books, following the shouting incident at lunch yesterday. I'm cringing as I write this. What was I thinking? I told them I was a **"shifty"**, went on about the hotness of the reynold ryans, and talked about my love of Squatties, but the more I tried, the clearer it was that I'm not "one of them". Cringe central! And then something happened that has **MOST CERTAINLY** put an end to any further friendship...

We were "hanging out" on the "cool" bench

(for clarity, no one seemed cold, and no one was hanging upside down) when Sophie screamed. And I mean like she was being murdered. A scream like someone who was being punished by Athena might scream. We all jumped up and hurried to her. She pointed to something on the ground – a spider.

ARACHNE?

No, even with my limited experience of spiders (just Arachne) I could tell this eight-legged creature was a bit different.  Olivia grabbed her shiny pink school bag, ready to hurl it at the defenceless creature and crush it. Even if this beastie wasn't my best friend, I couldn't let it be heartlessly squashed. I quickly knelt down and grabbed the spider, cupping it in my hands. It moved around lightly on my palm – not a terrible sensation.

I whispered to it, **"It's OK. You're safe with me."**

The other girls all looked horrified, like I'd eaten it or something. I took it carefully to the edge of the playground, where it wasn't likely to be disturbed, and let it go. By the time I returned to the bench, the other girls had gone. It was quite a clear message that I'd blown my chances to be part of their group. But I suddenly realized: even in the twenty-first century, I still need to be myself. And saving that spider made me miss my true friend Arachne. It's for her that I need to succeed in this task.

19:19

HOME, BEDROOM

On the way home tonight, I stopped by the well. I wish I could just jump into it and return to my own time. I wanted to see Arachne. Things were

much simpler in ancient Greece. And with all the gods around, you definitely knew where you stood.

I figured there wasn't any harm in whispering into the well. So I started saying, **"Arachne! Arachne, are you there? Can you hear me?"**

I knew it was pretty useless, but I could picture her gross furry body (no offence, Arachne), back there in ancient Greece, and I really wanted to make contact. Unfortunately, as I turned to leave, I saw Sophie and one of

the Os giggling at me. I don't really care if they think I'm weird. If it helps me be in contact with my friend, that's far more important than being pretend friends with anyone.

Things weren't much better at home. When I opened the door, I was confronted with a smell that nearly knocked me over, and jars that filled almost every room. There were more potions than at the witch Medea's palace! But that wasn't the most alarming part. Stheno and Euryale appeared, completely transformed. They have discovered **"MAKE-UP TUTORIALS"** on the internet. Bear in mind that I am just getting used to seeing my sisters in human form – but now they are caking themselves in orange goo. And

they have drawn eyebrows on their faces. I don't think they intended them to be so big. Or so wonky. They think they look great. I didn't have the heart to tell them otherwise.

THURSDAY 29 JUNE

12:54

SHADEWELL ACADEMY, GIRLS' TOILETS

School this morning has been both good and bad.

I'll come to the good news in a second – and it is VERY good news! But first, the bad:

I was sent to the head's office for a telling-off. There was a minor issue with something called PE – or physical education – which is what they call sports here. I'm very relieved to discover that there are now clothes for doing sport, but I only learnt this after blindfolding myself in order to prevent myself from seeing lots of twelve-year-old boys naked. In ancient Greece, all the boys do sport completely butt naked! **YUCK**. *No one wants to see that.* How was I supposed to know that they actually wear clothes these days?

Anyway, if that hadn't happened, I wouldn't have been sent to see the head. (Note: **"head"** is short for **"head teacher"**. Everyone calls them the head, but they do also have a body attached.) Shadewell Academy's head is called Ms Williams. She has her hair tied back in a tight bun and small glasses perched at the end of her nose. I think she's trying to look haughty - but she's got nothing on Athena. She had apparently heard about all my **"difficulties"** in fitting in to my new school. She said she had tried to **"cut me some slack"** but that she had received several reports from a range of staff and pupils about my "bizarre" behaviour. One more problem and I'll get "detention" apparently (whatever that means).

As Ms Williams talked, my eyes wandered over to a cabinet full of shiny objects – lots of trophies in the shape of cups and plates. Which brings me to the **GOOD NEWS:**

There, nestled at the back, taking up the height and width of the cabinet, was Athena's shield! I couldn't believe my eyes. I would recognize this object anywhere, having spent endless days with nothing to do other than stare at it **(or clean blood and gore from it)** – the intricate leaf pattern round its edge, the intertwined sea creatures forming a ring round the surprisingly plain centre.

By the time I left Ms Williams's office, I had two things: a plan to retrieve Athena's shield by stealing it from this very unsecure cabinet and a **"FINAL WARNING"**.

KOMOS

HOME, ~~BEDROOM, KITCHEN, THE ORACLE'S ROOM,~~ BEDROOM. I CAN'T STAY STILL – I'M TOO EXCITED!

The most amazing thing has happened! I saw a message from Arachne!

An actual message!

Somehow her web message made it through Hades' well! It simply said:

She must be at the other end of the well, waiting for me to return!

HELLO! I HEAR YOU!

I hurriedly whispered down the well that I'd found the shield and that, later tonight, I will be getting it back. So I shouldn't be gone for

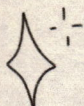

much longer – then we'll both be returned to our normal states.

Stheno and Euryale looked even more ridiculous when I returned home. But they seem to be having fun, so who am I to judge? They now have things called "cameras" set up in the living room, so they can record themselves doing their make-up and make those magical moving pictures that everyone seems to like so much at school. At least fluffy cat videos are cute – I don't know why anyone would want to watch two people applying really bad make-up. But my sisters are determined to become something called "influencers". What is that? Is that a job? If pointlessly guarding a shield for an all-powerful god is a job, I suppose anything can be!

I did manage to stop my sisters staring at themselves through mirrors and phones long enough to tell them about finding the shield and my plan to break into the school tonight. They've promised to help me. We'll break in when the sky is at its darkest, so we're least likely to be seen. Hopefully, by this time tomorrow, we'll all be home in ancient Greece.

FRIDAY 30 JUNE

01:47

STILL IN THE TWENTY-FIRST CENTURY

Well, that was **A BUST**.

We didn't even get through the school gates! There were two cars with blue flashing lights pulled up outside, and lots of people – all called **"officer"** – all dressed the same, and speaking to each other on small chunky boxes which were attached to their shoulders.

I asked one of the "officers" what was happening, and she said, **"The police received a tip-off about a planned break-in at the school tonight. It was an odd thing — we got a video sent in of two people who appeared to be disguised as clowns. But we couldn't tell who they were because the video was grainy. It might be nonsense, but you have to take these things seriously. You three get off home now."**

Very strange. People dressed as clowns trying to sabotage our plan? We had no chance of getting the shield tonight and, for now, we're still stuck here. I should feel angry about this, but it is a basic setback. And, actually, it was kind of cool doing something with my sisters, even if the mission didn't work out this time. I know where the shield is and I just need a bit more of a plan to get it. I'm feeling so calm and positive about it that my snake hair has barely been bothering me this evening.

Hang on a tick, everyone. I think we just missed something.
Huh?
Medusa had found the shield and was about to get it, but it sounds like someone sabotaged her plan.
Oh, cute little KITTIES.
You lot? Hey! Are you even listening to me?
Totally. LOL.
Of course. Smiley face.
What does that even mean?
About three o'clock.
OK, so you're really not paying attention. This is INFURIATING! The shield was right there – but someone called the police and stopped her getting it.
No way! That's awful.
Oh good, you are finally listening…
It's awful that my latest post only got three likes.
Is no one wondering who told the police?

HOME, KITCHEN

I got up this morning, determined to work out a new plan to retrieve the shield. Maybe by tonight I could be back with a human-form Arachne. Wouldn't that be amazing? I thought I'd just need to get through a fairly normal **(what is normal?)** day at school - but that did not quite go to plan.

I'd been told that Fridays in school involved collective worship.

I was prepared.

I was ready.

I wanted to make a good impression and take along a really good tribute as a sacrifice during worship - so I'd asked Oracle Alexa for a goat a couple of days ago.

Even as I walked into school, with the goat

trotting along beside me, I suspected I had made some kind of error. Everyone was staring at me. In fact, they even looked up from their phones to stare. Some of them started making their own magic moving pictures – sorry, **VIDEOS** – of the very confused goat.

Ms Williams met me at the entrance and ushered me straight to her office, telling me to tie up the goat outside. She started saying something about collective worship needing to be taken seriously, but I was distracted by the empty cabinet – Athena's shield was gone!

"Are you actually listening, Meddy?" she asked.

I clearly wasn't. I pointed to the cabinet.

"Yes, pupils bringing in animals is not the

only difficult thing I've had to deal with this morning. Last night, we were informed of an intended break-in, so we've had to lock the silverware safely away in the basement vault. No one will be getting them from there! Such a shame, though. It's so aspirational for pupils coming to my office to see the awards they can achieve if they apply themselves."

Then Ms Williams looked out of the window at my goat, who was now chewing on the rose bushes

that lined the building. "Of course some pupils come to my office for less ... positive reasons. This is the second time you've been here after only a week at our school. I understand this is all new to you, but we have **rules** and it is important that you learn to fit in. Next week, if this continues, I'll have no choice but to give you **detention**." Ms Williams was speaking kindly, and she didn't appear to be cross, but this felt like a bad thing. "For now, take that animal home and there's no need for you to come back for the rest of the day. Have a relaxing week-end and let's have a fresh start on Monday morning, yes? Any questions?"

"Yes. One. What's a **week-end?**"

So here I am back at home. This is such a confusing place. Hades says it's terrible and godless, but I've done loads of things wrong, and the teachers have been nice to me. I haven't witnessed anyone being stolen away by a demigod, or turned into a new type of beastie, or being attacked by monsters. Doesn't that make this place ... better?

Better or not, there's still lots I don't understand. Like why would teachers not want a goat as a tribute in collective worship? Everyone loves a goat! I've tied the goat up in our back garden, and it's munching on the plants out there, so now I'm going to see if I can communicate more with Arachne.

HERMES EXPRESS
AIR TORTOISE (H.E.A.T.)
OFFICIAL CORRESPONDENCE BETWEEN
HADES AND ATHENA

Hades,

I really don't think this is what I was promised when I signed that contract. I was trusting you to observe the situation and report back to me. But so far, nothing. Where is the suffering? Where is the PAIN? I've had enough. I may not be able to enter that world, but I can still use my powers to let Medusa know I am DISPLEASED.

On a more positive note, my design for your well is coming on beautifully. I'm thinking Doric columns, a Greek key pattern, and — my own special flourish — garlands of olive branches.

Athena

15:42

HOME AND SAFE – FOR NOW

That was a close one.

And I mean, **REALLY CLOSE.**

I'm fine.

I'm fine.

It's over now.

I *think* I just got a warning from Athena.

I thought the agreement was that the gods couldn't come and mess around with things here in the twenty-first century, but she's found a way to send a message. **Loud and clear.**

I spent this afternoon at Hades' well, having a great time catching up with Arachne. Actually, I'm not sure you can really describe it as catching up, but I was talking through the well, and she was sending occasional web updates such as

WOW (AND) AMAZING

as I told her all the things I'd learnt here.

I was just explaining about the delay with retrieving the shield, when a rumbling noise came from deep within the well. At first I thought Arachne was doing a long fart **(can spiders fart?)** but the sound continued, becoming louder and more ... **FLAPPY.** Soon the noise was so loud, people were coming out of buildings to see what was going on. Euryale and Stheno appeared at the corner of the square, phones in hand, ready to capture any action.

Suddenly, a flock – no, a **SWARM** – of owls burst out of the well. Hundreds of them. They swooped up into the sky, then flew down and started swirling around the well, the square and the school. Even the most phone-obsessed students rushed out of the school building and looked up into the sky, staring at the dark cloud of birds as they moved in unison.

I waited for the screaming and running to start – surely these twenty-first-century humans would consider this event a **TERRIBLE OMEN?** Surely they would be terrified and confused at the sight of nocturnal animals acting in this way?

I wasn't terrified. I was angry. I tried to

fight the feeling but it was burning within my chest. My brain was chanting **"I'm fine, I'm fine"** over and over again, but my body was taking over and the snakes were writhing round my head like never before. And why were the owls affecting me like this? Well, you see, I **KNEW** they were a message from Athena. Owls – Athena's favourite bird, a symbol of her wisdom – had been sent through the portal to let me know that the goddess of war was not happy. She was letting me know that she still has power over me.

As the owls flew faster and faster, forming a thundering tornado in the sky, I stood up and screamed. The scream was swallowed by the loud noise of the owls, but it helped my anger subside and, as it left my body, the owls also emptied from the sky, disappearing as quickly as they had appeared.

I waited, fearing that Athena's masking spell had slipped and that, any second now, someone would notice my hideous head of snakes – but I caught a glimpse of my reflection in a window, and breathed a sigh of relief to see normal hair. Phew. That was a close one. I wondered if Athena had sent the owls on purpose to try to blow my cover.

To be fair, even if my snake hair had been revealed, I'm not sure anyone would have noticed. Everyone was absolutely **buzzing** about what they'd just witnessed. By this time, it seemed like the whole school had emptied out. Sophie and the Os walked past me and I overheard Sophie saying, "Can you believe that? It must be some kind of advert for a new Harry Potter thing!"

"Harry WHO?" I asked.

Olivia laughed. "Wow, Meddy. You're so **weird.**"

Sophie and Olivia moved on, and I was left with even more questions. I tried to find my sisters in the throng of people, but could only see them in the distance, excitedly talking in their phones.

I'm not weird.

The twenty-first century is weird.

KOMOS

HOME, BEDROOM. IN THE TWENTY-FIRST CENTURY – FOR NOW

Terrible news.

I've found a (snake) in my hair.

This must mean that Athena's masking spell is failing. Did the owls cause this? Did my angry scream cause this?

One thing gives me hope, though. I haven't been whisked back to my time, so maybe this does not count as failing my task. Luckily, I have enough normal hair for this one snake to hide in, so perhaps I've got away with it. But it shows I need to be more careful with my emotions – or speed up with getting the shield back to Athena.

21:33

HOME, THE ORACLE ALEXA'S ROOM - AKA THE ROOM OF DEVASTATION

First the owls, then the snake ... and now this. The goat has **EATEN** the Oracle Alexa! It must have wandered into the living room while I was at the well, and I only noticed when I went to ask her about Harry Potter but found only the goat and some fragments of Oracle Alexa. I do hope we're not punished for this. **I can't take any more today!**

RIP ALEXA

Conversely, Stheno and Euryale are **DELIGHTED** at how today has gone. As they were first on the scene with their phones, they got really good videos of the owls and now have a large following on

170

"social media". They have relaunched themselves as influencers **Tina** and **Gail**, and are trending and "so hot* right now". They've been chatting non-stop about **"LIKES"** and **"DMs"** and **"brand awareness"**. They have even been contacted by companies for some big tie-ins. All this is great news, apparently, but after last night I'd hoped we could continue spending time together and now they're mega-focused on this. And I honestly have no idea what any of what they're talking about means – it's all nonsense and even writing it down is not making it make any more sense. I guess I'm pleased for them, but it doesn't help me or my task. Honestly, it's like my sisters couldn't care less if we stayed here forever.

The goat is now back in the garden, thinking about what he has done ... while eating the bushes.

*Why are people obsessed with hotness here? Is it because England is so cold?

HERMES EXPRESS
AIR TORTOISE (H.E.A.T.)
OFFICIAL CORRESPONDENCE BETWEEN
HADES AND ATHENA

H·E·A·T

My dearest and most alarmingly agitated Athena,

And WHAT exactly was that?

Hades

H·E·A·T

Hades,

Just a reminder to Medusa that I am here, waiting patiently. I was expecting more suffering. Or to have my shield back by now. I really expected more from you, Hades.

A

H·E·A·T

Dearest, dearest Athena,

Things work differently here. I was about to start with the torture in earnest and now you might have set back the whole punishment. Don't worry. I'll smooth things over and really get some grade-A pain going for Medusa. You'll receive reports that will make you very happy soon. Trust me!

You focus on decorating my well. Your design sounds wonderful.

Hades

Hades,

Ha! I never trust you. And, besides, I think you'll find that my little owl stunt has proved that your contract is defective. Doesn't it say that no other creatures from ancient Greece can enter the twenty-first century?

A

My dearest and most intelligently observant Athena,

A mere glitch. Nothing to concern yourself with. Now, about this well design, what material were you considering? Marble is nice. Or porphyry is very popular this year.

Hades

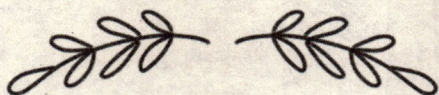

SATURDAY 31 JUNE

10:26

HOME, IN THE SAFETY OF MY BEDROOM – FOR NOW

Isn't it strange that there are such things as **weekends** here? And who decided that a week should be seven days long? That seems like a very odd number to pick. At least they don't have to keep thinking up names for days. It is sensible to keep recycling them. I can't believe that humans get actual days off now. I had to guard Athena's shield day in, day out. People here are so lucky. It seems as though the gods have no powers over them. They certainly don't go about their lives fearful of punishments.

So why did Hades choose this place for MY punishment? Why does he think this will be torture for me? Until I understand that, I have to be careful. And, most vitally, I have to control my temper until I can re-find the shield.

Still, that realization does not help me with my now visible snake-in-my-hair problem. I finally got Stheno and Euryale – sorry, Tina and Gail – off their phones long enough to show them the snake and do you know how they reacted?

They squealed and clapped and, both in unison, exclaimed, **"MAKEOVER!"**

Oh no!

HOME, KITCHEN

I have spent this afternoon being prodded and preened by my sisters, and now I am as orange as them. I did, thankfully, manage to persuade them not to create a video of my makeover. I definitely can't risk anyone seeing the snake in my hair if Gail and Tina posted the video **"ONLINE"**.

As much as I resent the whole snake thing, and being forced into this situation in the first place, it was quite fun to spend some time with my sisters. Even though we're now all human, we still don't have

much in common, but they were at least trying to help me out. And it's impressive how much they've learnt in just a week in the twenty-first century.

By the end of the day I looked **UTTERLY RIDICULOUS**, but smelled better,* and definitely felt calmer and, I think, happier. Maybe my sisters are helpful after all?

*I've noticed, since arriving here, that I'm starting to smell quite ... grim. I've never smelled this way before, so can only put it down to being part of Athena's punishment. Maybe it's the snakes that smell? Although that doesn't really explain why the smell is mainly coming from my armpits.

SUNDAY 32 JUNE

08:06

HOME, BEDROOM, HIDING (AGAIN)

Oh dear, I spoke too soon. When I opened my eyes this morning, I saw Gail's grinning face looming over me. Apparently my makeover is not complete. Yesterday, my sisters focused on my outward appearance, but today they want to help me learn how to relax and love myself (they were sounding a bit like the Oracle

Alexa - **oh, I miss Oracle Alexa!**).

They have a whole day planned out.

This is going to be hideous.

16:16

HOME, BEDROOM, STILL/AGAIN (TRYING TO AVOID MY SISTERS)

So my sisters have used the **"internet"** to become experts on how I should deal with my anger and stay calmer. They have been thorough - I'll give them that!

Some of the things actually worked - and, amazingly, top of their list of things to do was to **"write a journal"**. **HA!** I already do that!

I can't wait to tell Arachne that her suggestion is now the top *TRIED-AND-TESTED METHOD* for **"processing your emotions"**. Hang

on a sec – did she invent that?

My sisters also suggested that I should list the things that cause me anger and annoyance. Interesting. I will try that.*

Hmmm. Not sure it's really helping, but it was worth a try.

Anyway, the other things my sisters have had me trying today have been:

*It annoys me when my sisters try to tell me how to control my anger.

I. EXERCISING
It annoys me when my sisters make me go for a walk

2. DOING SOMETHING CREATIVE
It annoys me when I have to waste time painting a seascape. It annoys me when my sisters try to persuade me that applying make-up (orange goo) is a form of creativity.

3. LAUGHING
Don't feel there is much to laugh about here. Unless laughing at my sisters' make-up counts?

4. HAVING A MANTRA
It turns out I do this already. I've been telling myself "I'm fine" all week. I was self-soothing! Who knew? I might try to introduce other mantras if these work. My sisters talked a lot about letting my anger go.

5. FORGIVING PEOPLE

Exactly who am I supposed to be forgiving? Athena? Definitely not. **NO WAY.**

6. COUNTING DOWN

It annoys me when I am told to try counting down by my sisters who can't even count UP – ~~why should they get to tell me what and~~ 10, 9, 8, 7, 6, 5, 4, 3, 2, 1. Actually, that did help!

7. TALKING TO A FRIEND

I do this one already too! Talking to Arachne through the well has definitely helped keep me calm. I can't wait for her to be human again. In the meantime, it might be nice to have another friend. Not that I can really share anything about myself with them ~~when I have these stupid rules written into that blasted contract that the god~~ ... and 10, 9, 8, 7, 6, 5, 4, 3, 2, 1.

8. TAKING A BREAK

Just HOW am I supposed to take a break, when I have a time-limited mission to save my friend? Tell me that. How? ~~This is all just ridic–~~ and 10, 9, 8, 7, 6, 5, 4, 3, 2, 1. Ahhhh.

9. BREATHING

It annoys me when my sisters try to tell me how to breathe. They've only just stopped using gills! Plus I do this already. It is actually calming. It is annoying when my sisters suggest something that is actually useful.

You'd have thought this was plenty for one day, but my sisters don't want to stop there. No, they apparently have one more thing in store for me.

KOMOS

21:15

HOME, THE ORACLE ALEXA'S OLD ROOM

And 10, 9, 8, 7, 6, 5, 4, 3, 2, 1.

And breathe. In. Out. In. Out.

And laugh. **Ha ha ha.**

And let it go.

I'm fine.

OK, so I'm not fine. I'm really WOUND UP.

I have been going along with my sisters' silly plans all weekend.

Make-up. Shopping. Painting. A long walk around Shadewell was not my idea of fun **(NOT relaxing — why are all vehicles in the twenty-first century so noisy? I miss the gentle clip-clopping of donkeys),** but I did it because Gail and Tina **THOUGHT** it might help. In fact, all I feel is overstimulated.

But this latest thing?

This is a step too far.

For their final part of the plan, they'd rearranged Oracle Alexa's old room (RIP Oracle Alexa) with blankets draped over the floor and cushions scattered around. We were having lots of fun painting each other's nails (well, not that fun for me) and Gail and Tina were busy plaiting each other's hair, when Tina suggested I get comfortable with my new hair too. Gail encouraged me to sit on the cushions, and look into the free-standing mirror.

And can you guess what they wanted me to do?

They wanted me to **"get to know"** my snake.

How silly is that?

They thought I should **spend some time** with it.

They wanted me to **talk** to it.

They think that this snake is actually **part of me!**

They even wanted me to **NAME** it.

Of all ~~the stupid...~~

And 10, 9, 8, 7, 6, 5, 4, 3, 2, 1.

I don't want to get to know **ANY** snake, let alone the one sticking out of the back of my head. The only reason this snake is part of me is because of Athena. I will not be having **ANYTHING** to do with a snake, thank you very much. The best thing I can do is ignore this one that broke through Athena's masking spell.

Now that I've got more methods to calm my anger, I won't have any problem with the other snakes. I just need to focus on finding the shield and getting back home. End of.

Tomorrow, when this endless week-end finally finishes, I can get back into school and do what I'm here to do – save Arachne.

MONDAY 3 JULY*

┌─────────────┐
│   13:17   │
└─────────────┘

SHADEWELL ACADEMY, GIRLS' TOILETS

Right, new school week and new focus. I **HAVE** to get to the shield. The good news is that I know where the shield is - it's in the basement of the school. The bad news is that the basement is out of bounds, and I have no idea how to get to it.

After the horrors of the weekend, I'd almost

forgotten about the horrors of school. I was totally OK with heading into school friendless and alone (**I'd passed by the well and seen a cheery message from Arachne, which helped**), so imagine my surprise when Sophie and the Os were hanging around the entrance, waiting for me.

It turns out that Gail and Tina are now **celebrities**, and people are interested in **ME** because of **THEM**. Eh? How does that work? I'm still the same person as last week. It's actually been quite difficult to ditch **"SOOO"**. It's like they expected me to be delighted that they wanted to be my friends. But at first break, on the cool bench, I was frozen with boredom. The only thing those girls seemed interested in doing was staring at the boys kicking a ball around, and occasionally flicking their hair over their shoulders, like they were horses trying to get rid of flies. When I tried to leave them to it, they gave me little sad **pouty faces with big eyes*** – as if me not being with them was the **WORST** thing that could ever happen. I found myself feeling jealous of Inna – the friendly-looking girl with the heavy fringe – who was just sitting calmly by herself reading a book. She doesn't look bothered about fitting in. That's how I need to be!

*These faces annoy me.

20:54

HOME, EXHAUSTED!

My new plan for finding another way into the basement and locating the shield is to try to get out of class as much as possible, so I can snoop the corridors while everyone else is in lessons. The problem is, I don't really know which teachers will let me out of class. It's very much a **trial-and-error** thing.

In Miss Carlton's art class, we were making clay pots. I'm actually great at these, and had already churned out several by the time most of the class were still making the sides of their first one, so she "let me get something from my locker". I don't even know what a locker is, but I've heard the other children mention them. I managed to scout along one full corridor without being seen – but sadly got no further forward with finding a way down to the basement.

In Mr Philson's* science lesson, however, we were learning about "digestion". I was trying to keep my head down and not answer any questions wrong (he already thinks I'm a fool), but I **HAVE** to get to the basement, so when everyone was told to start working in their books, I approached his desk to ask if I could go to the toilet.

*It annoys me when Mr Philson's nose whistles.

"Is it **'GIRLS' PROBLEMS'**"? he asked, loud enough for everyone to hear.

I didn't really know how to answer that. I'm not sure it is specifically **"GIRL"** problems that mean I have been cursed with a head of snakes by a powerful Greek god and been tasked to retrieve a shield from a different time and place, so I simply said, **"No!"**

Mr Philson looked very relieved at this, and said, "In that case, I suggest you learn from this lesson today, and take better control of your digestive system. You can use the toilet at the end of the day."

He beamed around the room, like he'd been hilarious,* and the children sniggered. I could feel my cheeks flush with embarrassment as I walked back to my desk with everyone looking at me.

To make things **EVEN WORSE**, I tried to say a mantra under my breath, to calm myself

* It annoys me when teachers try to humiliate their pupils. Is this part of Hades' punishment?

down. **"Let it go. Let it go,"** I was repeating to myself.

Suddenly, Oscar **(aka Sophie's crush)** shouted, "Ugh! Meddy's just said she'd **'Let one go'!** Meddy's farted. That's disgusting!"

And then the whole class erupted, making vomiting noises and claiming they could smell my fart. Sophie was shaking her head in a disappointed way, as if my humiliation was somehow bringing shame upon her, or perhaps that my **"FART"** had somehow tainted her crush.

More anger was rising within me, and all I could do as I sat down was breathe deeply, praying that the moment would pass. If I could survive Athena's owls, I could survive a class of children guffawing at me.

"That's right," Oscar said loudly, so everyone could hear. "Breathe it in deeply – it'll help get rid of it for the rest of us."

In the name of Zeus, I would like to take Oscar's head ~~and smash it into the~~ ... and 10, 9, 8, 7, 6, 5, 4, 3, 2, 1.

So that was not an ideal end to the day - but, on the plus side, it turns out that if you fart in class (side note: I totally **DID NOT** fart in class), you tend to lose a bit of kudos with the popular girls. **Phew!** Hopefully now they'll leave me alone. Isn't it amazing how easily someone can go from being flavour of the month to an outcast so quickly at secondary school? It makes my head spin!

HERMES EXPRESS
AIR TORTOISE (H.E.A.T.)
OFFICIAL CORRESPONDENCE BETWEEN
HADES AND ATHENA

H·E·A·T

My dearest and most satisfyingly sadistic Athena,

I'm delighted to report that Medusa is really starting to feel the pain now.

Hades

H·E·A·T

Dear Hades,
That's fantastic news. It's about time. What's happening to her? I demand more detail!

A

My dearest and most incorrigibly inquisitive Athena,

Oh, it's torture. Absolute torture. Currently being chased by a pack of snarling hounds.

Hades

Splendid! That's more like it.

A

TUESDAY 4 JULY

13:21

SHADEWELL ACADEMY, UNDER A TREE

SUCCESS! I have found the door to the basement! It's not the one that Sophie pointed out on my first day – that one is always locked (I've checked). No, this one accesses the basement from **THE STAFFROOM!** I found it this morning, when I was supposed to be in a history lesson with Mr Warburton.*

*Mr Warburton's coffee breath annoys me.

I was actually finding the lesson interesting, learning about the strange place called America and how people there had fought to make the rules themselves and stand up for their own rights. Wouldn't that be a wonderful thing? Not to be ruled by all-powerful beings? **BUT**, however interesting the lesson, I had to focus on **MY MISSION**.

I told Mr Warburton loudly that I was having **"GIRLS' PROBLEMS"** and he couldn't give me permission to leave his classroom fast enough. I'm still not sure what "girls' problems" are, but the teacher didn't appear to need any further detail, so I'm just pleased to have found something that gets me out of class! If only I'd said yes to Mr Philson, when he asked yesterday.

The staffroom was empty and quiet – except for the **drip, drip, drip** of a tap, dripping on

to a pile of dirty cups in the sink. A note was stuck by the sink, which read **DO YOUR OWN WASHING-UP!!!! MS W.** I guess the teachers have rules too. But clearly not one about the number of exclamation marks it is appropriate to use.

There were several doors in the staffroom. One clearly led outside, as it was labelled **FIRE EXIT**, but it also had a notice in big red letters, saying **DO NOT USE THIS AS AN EXIT!!!!!! Ms W.** I tried another door, behind which a huge machine was churning away, spitting out bits of identically decorated paper. The final door opened on to stairs heading downwards – the **BASEMENT!** I peered into the darkness. The glow of dim electric lights showed me that the basement was vast – I think it must go under the whole school – but I couldn't see beyond where the corridor turned a corner.

It must be like a labyrinth! I didn't have time to explore more because I heard shouting from outside the staffroom. Do teachers get training in how to shout so loudly? Even Hermes, messenger of the gods, was quieter than that, when he came down from Mount Olympus with announcements from Zeus!

Unfortunately, the shouting teacher turned out to be Ms Williams!!!! I had just enough time to move away from the door to the basement, but not enough time to find a hiding spot, so I was caught standing gormlessly in the centre of the staffroom. **Whoops!**

"What are you doing in here?" demanded the head.

"Erm, girls' problems?"

"Oh, right," said Ms Williams quite brusquely. "Well, you can't be in here. And you were skating on thin ice as it was. Being in the staffroom is **automatic detention**, I'm afraid. Mr Philson will be expecting you in the detention room at the end of the day. And here" – she rummaged in a cupboard marked **"+"** for something – **"take this."**

I had no idea what to do with the squashy white parcel she'd handed to me, but I didn't want to admit that, so I just nodded. It must be something to do with detention.

Detention, as far as I can tell, means I just have to sit in a room with other children who haven't **"followed the rules"**, for a short amount of time after school finishes. What a waste of time! I've only got a limited number of days to find the shield and now I know how to get into the basement, I don't want to be stuck in detention. I know in the grand scheme of things it's not like – oh, I don't know – being turned into a **SPIDER** or anything. But I have important things to be getting on with!

Sophie and the Os reacted like detention was the **WORST** thing imaginable and I have, once more, been cast out of their group. I wouldn't mind so much, but now that I'm officially not "one of them", I've been hearing them talk about me behind my back – because my uniform isn't right. Isn't the point of a uniform that we all wear the same thing? I think my clothes look the same as everyone else's.

I've even got to grips with zips (ha, that rhymes). But no. Apparently, you are only acceptable as a human being if you wear shirts that look, from a distance, like **EVERY OTHER WHITE SHIRT**, but that if you examine very closely, you see a small squiggle embroidered IN WHITE at the corner of the pocket, which apparently means it's from a special shop.* **WHAT IS THE POINT OF THAT?**

I think I'm starting to understand why Hades sent me here. I thought I was getting used to it here, but there just seems to be so much to consider, and very little of it makes sense. Not only are there the school rules (which, seemingly, the teachers do not have to follow) and the things you have to learn about at school, but there are also the social rules made up by goodness knows who. Maybe America had the right idea to draw up a proper constitution. I bet everyone is so happy there that there are never any problems. But it's very difficult

*It annoys me when people judge others based on rules that they've just made up.

to do the right thing all the time here — so I've decided not to worry too much about it. In fact, right now, I'm flouting a rule that Sophie told me on my second day here: not going anywhere near Inna. I saw her sitting alone again this lunchtime, reading, so I joined her. We've been sitting quietly together — her reading and me writing this. It definitely beats hiding in the toilet!

HERMES EXPRESS
AIR TORTOISE (H.E.A.T.)
OFFICIAL CORRESPONDENCE BETWEEN HADES AND ATHENA

H·E·A·T

My dearest and most artfully vengeful Athena,

You will be delighted to hear that Medusa is barely hanging on. I wouldn't be surprised if she snaps at any moment and breaks your masking spell. Those snakes are aching to be released — I can tell. You really should feel sorry for her. The poor girl will almost certainly fail in her mission.

Hades

Hades,

Nonsense! It sounds like she's only suffering as I wanted her to suffer. If she surprises us and gets my shield back, I will honour the contract. I will return her and her friend to their normal selves. But I am pleased that your punishment is finally coming together. I thought you'd lost your touch for a moment!

A

Me, my dearest and most maleficent Athena? Never!

Hades

Hades is doing it **again**.

Medusa is doing fine. She's writing in her diary, processing her emotions and using the different methods her sisters suggested — plus she's getting closer to finding the shield. She's getting on great.

So what is Hades talking about?

And why?

HOME, AND IN TROUBLE

So, it turns out that if you don't tell your sisters that you're going to be late home because of detention, they get a bit annoyed. When they have made your dinner and it's sitting cold on the table, they look at you accusingly, like you did it on purpose. And when you say "Why are you being like this? You're not my mum!" that also does not go down well. Actually, I don't know why I said that last bit – it's not like Mum ever made dinner **(you know, being a cave-dwelling sea monster and all)**.

So I tried to apologize to them. It was inconsiderate, I suppose, not letting them know I was going to be late. But it was my first detention. I didn't know how these things worked. I did try to make them happier by informing them that I now know how to access the basement, so the shield is as good as ours. They didn't perk up at that. If anything they got even grumpier. I guess they're still annoyed at me.

It might be something to do with me already having detention for tomorrow as well (but at least they know about that one in advance – progress!). It turns out that whatever Ms Williams handed me in the staffroom was NOT part of detention. So when I walked into the silent detention classroom and handed it to Mr Philson, he was NOT impressed. He went pink, and then red, and then, amazingly, bright purple. Beads of sweat appeared on his forehead and he wiped them off with his hand. I nearly suggested using the spongy rectangular parcel he had in his hand – it does seem like it would be good for absorbing liquids – but something told me it was not the time to offer that bit of advice. Instead, I nodded wordlessly as Mr Philson told me I had a **detention again** tomorrow, and hurried to sit down. At least I know not to take another rectangular spongy parcel tomorrow!

Detention itself was boring and uneventful. I just had to sit there and **"think about what I had done"**. Well, this was really useful! Free time to think about how to access the basement in order to find the shield – as a punishment? That's basically what I should be spending my ENTIRE time here thinking about, and not having to learn about faraway places (America), embarrassingly simple crafts that a three-year-old should know (clay pots) or weird new explanations for how the body works. Honestly, if the gods had wanted us humans

to know about how food travels through our bodies, they'd have put all our tubey things on the outside. Anyway, I think I've come up with a plan. As long as I can get my sisters on board (I may have to ask for some make-up to be applied this evening – that'll make them happy) we'll try to get into the basement tomorrow night.

I wasn't the only pupil in detention this evening. There was a slightly older boy sitting at the back of the classroom. Mr Philson just ignored him but, to be fair, the boy wasn't paying any attention to anything but himself. He had his phone on selfie mode and was just staring at himself in various different poses for the entire detention. To give the boy his due, I could totally see why he kept staring at himself. I don't think I've ever seen anyone so handsome.

No – so **beautiful**. But he **DEFINITELY** knows it! Mr Philson seemed to realize it was useless to ask the boy – Narcy, I think he was called – to put the phone away, so the teacher just told him to sit quietly and that he'd see him the same time tomorrow and every other day until he stopped endlessly gawping at himself.

The third and final pupil in detention was a girl who looked like she was in maybe Year 10 or 11. Mr Philson actually spoke really nicely to this other girl. While I was plotting how to get the shield, I couldn't help but overhear what he was saying. The girl was sitting there, absolutely refusing to let go of a grotty-looking box.

"Now, Dora," Mr Philson was saying, "I know you're new, but you have to understand that there are rules at this school, and you can't be going around with personal items like this. If it's that

precious to you, then leave it at home."

"Oh, I can't do that," said Dora, starting to blub. "There'll be untold horror and misery."

"OK, OK. How about we get you sorted with a locker? Would that work?"

"Oh no, sir. I have to keep it with me," Dora responded, clutching the box to her chest even more desperately.

Dora, Dora, Dora, I kept thinking. The name rang a bell, but I couldn't think what it reminded me of.

I drifted in and out of their conversation. Mr Philson was trying really hard to be considerate, but by the end he seemed to have run out of options. Dora will be getting detentions for as long as it takes her to give up the box. I wonder what's in it. Still, the good news is there'll be people I know in detention tomorrow!

As my sisters continued to sulk this evening,

I went to Hades' well to tell Arachne the good news. I can't wait for us to be reunited.

KOMOS

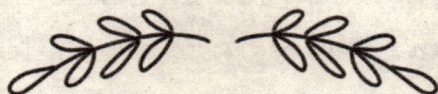

WEDNESDAY 5 JULY

13:02

SHADEWELL ACADEMY, UNDER A TREE AGAIN

I'm sitting with Inna again this lunchtime. Like yesterday, she is reading her book and I am writing this. It feels ... nice. No one is being mean or judgy. She's just easy to be with. For the first time since arriving here, I almost feel relaxed. My snakes are hardly bothering me at all.

Inna was waiting for me when I arrived this morning and gave me a friendly smile – which was the exact opposite of the icy stare I received from Sophie and the Os. If looks could kill! I don't get it: they don't want to be friends with me (which is TOTALLY fine), but they don't want me to be friends with someone else they don't want to be friends with?!

Anyway, **friendships, schmendships** – hopefully, by tonight, I will be **OUT OF HERE**. I just need to get through today and this afternoon's detention. Thinking about the shield has perhaps made me a bit distracted. I wasn't really paying attention in tutorial, which annoyed Miss Morley, but she was talking about the last one and a half weeks of the school year, which are completely irrelevant to me. She kept talking about **Tuesday 18 July** being the last day of term, which, funnily enough, would also be the last of my twenty-four days here – but as I'm getting that shield and leaving tonight, I don't need to know anything about that.

I was only vaguely aware of Miss Morley going on about some inter-house school competition, based on points given out to pupils through the year, that is apparently "very important", and which everyone should be "very excited about". The teacher was talking like her life depended on Austen House being successful. Apparently, the points were all super close this year, so we needed to "pull together", "pull our socks up" and "pull our fingers out". While she'd been droning on, I was going over my plan in my head. I only looked up when I realized she had stopped talking.

"Did you hear what I just said there, Meddy?"

I nodded.

"So what was I talking about?"

I had no idea. I'd stopped listening after the third pulling. But she clearly expected an answer and so I said the one thing that was in my mind.

"The shield."

"Hmmm. Lucky guess. Yes, correct."

Could it be that Athena's beloved and most prized possession is being used as the END-OF-YEAR PRIZE at Shadewell Academy?

Miss Morley then addressed the whole class. "So there'll be no letting up in these final days. Keep earning those points. Good behaviour and good work – that's what will win the shield for Austen House. Even if you've been working on stuff at home, bring it in – artwork, music, writing – these can all earn you extra points. But remember that you can lose points too, so don't let yourselves down. And try to avoid detention."

She was looking at me for that last bit.

But why should I care about some pointless inter-house school competition? There'll be no shield awarded for the inter-house school competition this year. By the time term ends, the shield and I will be long gone.

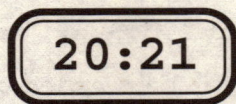

20:21

HOME, ALONE

Well, this is just annoying.

I got home from detention to find the house empty. I knew my sisters were sulking, but I'd **TOLD** them the plan about breaking into the basement tonight – so where are they?

Detention was basically the same as yesterday, with Narcy staring at himself, Dora refusing to let go of her box, me plotting to break into the school (although hopefully Mr

Philson doesn't know that) and another pupil. It was hard to miss this other kid. I don't think he'd got the information on school uniform, because he turned up in full gold: gold tracksuit, gold cap, gold trainers. It was quite a look! I didn't catch his name. I think he must have been learning about those tiny little things that people here call "GERMS", because he was refusing to touch anything with his hands. I guess, if you think about the idea of invisible-to-the-eye creatures too much, you really wouldn't want to touch anything either. Sometimes it's best not to know this stuff.

I don't know why, but all three of the other pupils in detention seem familiar. I've been trying to think who they remind me of. And

Mr Philson seemed to despair at all four of us. He gave a speech about how starting a new school should be an opportunity for a fresh start and a clean slate, and told us he was very disappointed to see four pupils who were all new to the school already in detention and struggling to follow the rules. If Mr Philson knew I was from ancient Greece, he might understand a bit better and cut me some slack – but it's not like I can tell him that. I have no idea what the other new pupils' excuses are for getting into trouble.

Ugh, I was hoping that by the time I'd written about detention, Gail and Tina would have turned up. I've even had to sort out my own dinner. Where are they? I can't believe they'd do this to me. They **knew** I needed their help tonight. OK, I'm really starting to get annoyed.*

Don't they even care about getting back to our own time? They must be missing their cave. It's just so rude. When they come back, I'm going to really ~~have a go at them and~~ ... and 10, 9, 8, 7, 6, 5, 4, 3, 2, 1.

Breathe.

Hmmm. Looks like my plan will have to take place tomorrow night instead.

Well, with them gone and no Oracle Alexa to talk to, I'm going to go to the well and catch up with Arachne. Hopefully she can calm me down a bit.

*It annoys me when I tell people what I need them to do and they don't do it.

221

KOMOS

222

THURSDAY 6 JULY,

$$\boxed{08:06}$$

HOME ALONE 2

Still no sign of my sisters this morning, although I think I know where they are. And I am NOT happy about it. I found an invitation to an **"Influencers Convention"** on the kitchen table, which is taking place today **AND TOMORROW**. If they have gone there, I will be so angry.

BREATHE.
IT'S FINE.
I'M FINE.

ATHENA HAPPY

Actually, I'm not fine. I went to Hades' well last night and was updating Arachne about everything. But the web updates I was getting back from Arachne were really confusing. She weaved things like 'Athena happy' and 'You failing'. What now? Am I failing? I thought I was getting close to succeeding. I **knew** I shouldn't trust these gods. At least they haven't sent any more owls.* Yet.

*Isn't it strange that no one has mentioned the owls since they happened? I guess people have so much to think about nowadays, like strange new lands and all the different disgusting squidgy organs in our bodies, that things just move on really quickly.

YOU FAILING

SHADEWELL ACADEMY,
UNDER OUR TREE

Not much time to update the diary now. Spent this lunchtime chatting to Inna instead. In some ways, she reminds me of Arachne. Maybe because she's the one person around here who doesn't seem to be judging others – she's just getting on with her own thing. She told me lots about herself and her family. Apparently, she only moved to England a year ago, because there was a terrible war in her own country. She said she still misses her old friends and her old way of life, but there is no way back for her and she is starting to like it here. No wonder we are becoming friends – I know this is different from my experience, but she understands what it is like to be in a strange new place.

HOME ALONE 3

Ooops. Third detention in a row! At least my sisters won't be annoyed at me getting home late and missing dinner, because they're still not back from their convention thingy. And breathe.

And this time the detention was totally not my fault. I was only trying to stand up for Inna, because Sophie and Ottilie were saying something mean about her earrings, and then a teacher got involved and I tried to explain the situation but he wouldn't listen and just talked over me, which was rude,* so I kept on trying to stand up for Inna, which **SOMEHOW** earned me another detention.

It was the usual suspects in detention again after school: me, Dora, Narcy and that golden boy. I thought that was it, but some really skinny lad appeared too – called Talus, I think. Apparently

*It annoys me when adults interrupt and don't listen to what a younger person has to say.

he'd been caught trying to steal food from the dinner hall. He came in saying, **"But I'm just starving."** To be fair, he did look really hungry, but Mr Philson wasn't in a sympathetic mood. I could hear Talus's stomach rumbling as he sat down across the aisle from me. I felt sorry for him, so I found a cereal bar in my bag, but I wasn't sure how to give it to him without annoying Mr Philson, so I just placed it on the ground and kicked it over to Talus. Sadly, I did not quite kick it in the right direction, so however hard he tried, Talus still couldn't reach it.

Anyway, I made up my mind about something: whether my sisters are back or not, tomorrow night, I **WILL** be getting into that basement and getting the shield.

HERMES EXPRESS
AIR TORTOISE (H.E.A.T.)

OFFICIAL CORRESPONDENCE BETWEEN
HADES AND ATHENA

My dearest and most delightfully bitter Athena,

Are you ready with your plans for Medusa? She'll be back here any day now. And my betting is she won't have your shield with her. That poor girl is really suffering. I'd be surprised if she comes back with all her limbs attached. Honestly, Athena, I think you'll struggle to top the punishments Medusa has been receiving.

Hades

Hades,

Are you questioning my punishment skills? Rude! Oh, I've known for as long as I've known Medusa just how she is going to be punished for all eternity. The snake hair is just the start. If she fails to bring my shield to me, I'll make her look so hideous that she'll wish she was never born.

A

FRIDAY 7 JULY

13:03

SHADEWELL ACADEMY,
UNDER OUR TREE

Inna has just asked me if everything is OK. To be honest, it's been quite a trying morning. I didn't have time to write earlier, because when I got up, my lovely hair was all greasy and disgusting. Apart from the obvious snake-hiding-in-hair problem, in all my twelve years my hair has never

looked anything other than glorious. So what fresh hell is this? Is this an extra punishment from the gods? That hardly seems fair. I felt exceedingly huffy about this as I washed it, and it made me late for school.

I mentioned my greasy hair to Inna, who just shrugged and said it's totally normal for girls our age. Really? Surely they're not all being punished by a vengeful goddess.

Anyway, Inna seemed to think there was something more bothering me. She said, **"I know how hard it is to start a new school. If there's anything you want to talk about, maybe I could help?"**

I guess I must seem a bit jittery because of my plan for tonight. But it's not like I could tell Inna

ANYTHING

about it. The contract was quite clear that if anyone finds out who I am, the mission will have failed and I'll be sent back to ancient Greece to be punished forever by an all-powerful god. And, worse than that, my best friend will remain a spider. I just mumbled that I was fine and now I am focused on writing this. Out of the corner of my eye, I can see Inna is a bit hurt. After all, she did share her story with me yesterday. But there's really nothing I can do!

21:54
HOME ALONE 4

Right. This is it. I'm just waiting for the middle of the night and then I will be heading into school.

I am still hoping Gail and Tina will walk through the door any moment now.

Nope.

Or now?

Nah.

Oh well.

But humans can only return through the well **WITH** the shield - so my sisters better be back soon. Once I have the shield, I really don't want to wait around much longer.

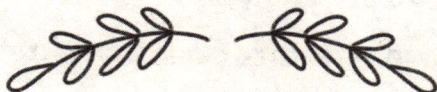

SATURDAY 8 JULY

04:03

HOME, BEDROOM – AND LIVID!

What a nightmare. What an absolute nightmare.

I can't believe the **SNEAKY, SLY** gods could do this.

Can I write fast enough to get my anger out?

Can I breathe deeply enough?

There are not enough numbers **IN THE WORLD** to count down from to ease my anger.

HOW COULD THEY?

We signed a contract. I thought the gods were going to play fair.

I was so close.

It had been going so well.

Even without my sisters' help, I made it into school and to the staffroom with absolutely no problems. The basement even still had the dim lights on, so I had no difficulty finding my way underground in the dark.

The basement was vast and maze-like, with corridors winding in every direction. I opened any door that I came across. Mainly there were just broken bits of old chairs, or stacks of identical books. But each door I opened was one door closer to finding the shield, so I kept going. At some point I got a bit lost and found myself opening doors to rooms I'd already looked in, but I managed to get back on track and cover all the basement except for the furthest corner.

As I approached the last area, my skin started to prickle. My snakes, having generally been fairly under control for the last few days, were now feeling uncomfortable on my head. And **THAT** was when I heard it.

It started with a strange breathing sound that, at first, I thought was coming from me. And I heard footsteps that weren't quite in sync with my own, but initially I thought my steps were simply echoing down the empty corridors. There was one door left to open. All I had to do was get to that door – but as I reached for the handle, a grunt came from the shadows.

I spun round.

TERROR.

I ran – no, sprinted – only looking back in

snatched glimpses. The creature – whatever it was – was chasing me through the basement. Each time it was illuminated by a dim green emergency light, I saw different features: large human feet; torn clothes; a hairy muscled chest; horns.

I don't know how I managed to make it back to the steps, but I powered up to the staffroom, trying to shove some of the low chairs in front of the door, and then burst out of the fire escape.

The panic in my chest is only just subsiding.

My breathing is only just returning to normal.

I *think* I'm safe – for now.

But just how am I supposed to get the shield if Hades and Athena do things like that?

HOME – AND NOT ALONE ENOUGH

OH NO. NO. NO. NO. NO.

Another snake!

A second snake has broken through Athena's spell.

This may be the worst day ever. And it's barely even started.

HOME, IN MY BEDROOM/IN A HUFF

I am trying to write this with no emotion, so that I don't cause further damage to Athena's masking spell.

So, my sisters are back.

They returned and apologized for missing going down to the basement.

I have accepted their apology.

I told them about my experience down there.

I described the monster that chased me.

Apparently, my sisters know this creature (they do not like the term "monster"). It is the **MINOTAUR** - half man, half bull. And, according to Gail and Tina, he is an absolute delight. Just a little misunderstood.

Misunderstood? He chased a terrified girl through a basement!

10, 9, 8, 7, 6, 5, 4, 3, 2, 1. And I'm writing calmly...

They are thrilled to know he is here and are determined to enter the school, bring him home and give him something called a **"GLOW UP"?**

I don't even want to know what that is.

I am wrapping my hair **(AND TWO SNAKES)** in a towel and going to chat to Arachne.

$$\boxed{19:20}$$

HOME, IN BED

There are days when I find myself longing for the boredom of looking after Athena's shield, back in the temple complex at the base of Mount Olympus. This is one of those days. I wish I'd never whinged about cleaning blood and gore off the shield. I wish I'd been kinder about my fellow brainless guardians. I wish I was back in that simple life.

Instead, these things have happened today:

#1 There is a creature called a Minotaur in my kitchen, being primped and preened by my sisters. So far, he has received a **"manny peddy"** (?), a haircut and some **facial hair "sculpting"**.

Tina is currently searching the internet for a hat big enough to cover his horns. But I suppose my sisters were right. When he's not chasing a screaming person along a corridor, he's actually quite pleasant. Gail says he just needs treating with kindness. We'll see.

#2 I chatted to Arachne, but I don't know if she's forgetting the letters I taught her or whether her web updates are becoming defective, because she's stopped making any sense. I told her about the Minotaur (or Jeremy, as he wants to be called) and how the gods must have sent him here. All she weaved in response was **"CONTRACT"** and then a dot. Maybe her spider brain works differently from a human brain?

#3 And while I was at the well, who did I bump into but Inna? She was a bit surprised by my hair-in-towel look, but not as shocked as I was when she said,

"Awwww, is that your pet?"

One of my snakes had wiggled free and was slithering round my shoulders!

Panicked, I could only think of agreeing – at least Inna couldn't see that the snake was actually **ATTACHED TO MY SKULL.** My panic made the snake hiss. Not great. The last thing I wanted was for Inna to be attacked. I gingerly patted the loose snake and said, **"There, there."** Amazingly, the snake responded to my touch and calmed down a bit.

"Best for you not to touch him," I said to Inna. "He's a bit nervous around new people."

"No worries. What's his name?" she asked.

My mind went blank. What was a sensible name for a snake? If only I'd named the stupid thing when my sisters had suggested it last weekend. But instead I'd got angry at their idea. **POO.** Inna was still looking at me, waiting.

I said the first thing I saw.

"Car."

"Your snake is called 'Car'?"

"Um, yes. 'Mr Car', actually."

So I now have a snake on my head called Mr Car.

This kind of thing never happened in ancient Greece.

SUNDAY 9 JULY

17:35

HOME, LIVING ROOM

I have spent today taking my sisters' advice and have been spending some time with the two snakes that are now visible under my hair. I hate to admit it but my sisters were probably right.* The snakes do seem to respond to being treated kindly. And I suppose my sisters were also right that these snakes are part of me – so the better

*Does this mean my sea-monster sisters are actually doing a decent job of acting as carers for me? Maybe I can be too quick to judge sometimes. Though does that make me as bad as the likes of the temple guardians and Sophie? Oh no!

I know them, the better I know myself.

Of course, I haven't completely taken my sisters' advice: I did not use candles or blankets or any nonsense like that. I just sat looking into a mirror, talking to the snakes in a soothing manner. And I feel better for it.

I don't know whether any of this will help me with the mission. If I lose my temper again and the masking spell breaks completely, my task here is over. But I think spending time with these two snakes has at least helped me know how to keep them hidden under my hair, while also keeping them calm and happy. Their names are Mr Car **(which has stuck)** and for the newer one I've picked a better name. One that sounds modern, exotic and sophisticated:

IAN.

Now that the Minotaur – sorry, Jeremy – is out of the basement, I should be able to get to the shield more easily. I thought this task was only going to take a day. Two at most. And here I am, fifteen days in. **FIFTEEN DAYS?** Can that be right? I've had over half my allotted time in this place. Even though I know where the shield is, and Jeremy is no longer guarding it, I don't think there's any point in feeling confident that I can just go and grab it. If there's anything the last few days have taught me, it's that the gods don't play fair.

HERMES EXPRESS
AIR TORTOISE (H.E.A.T.)
OFFICIAL CORRESPONDENCE BETWEEN HADES AND ATHENA

H·E·A·T

Hades,

Do I need to intervene again? You said Medusa would be failing any time now. You said she'd be back here with me. I want that girl. And I want my shield.

A

My dearest and most fetchingly
fretful Athena,

For an immortal, you really have very little patience.
Medusa is putting up a good fight but only just
managing to keep her temper. You should see the knots
she's tying herself in, fighting against everything I'm
throwing at her. It is SO much fun. You can't deny me a
little more fun, can you? You know how bored I am with
whiny dead humans. I'd forgotten how thrilling torturing
a live human can be! After all, there's still plenty of
time left on the contract that you agreed to.

Hades

Hades,

Humph. I'm beginning to regret ever agreeing
to this contract. Actually, I think I'd like to make a
change to it. And you wouldn't deny me that, would you?
I think I'd now like the contract to say that even if
Medusa SUCCEEDS in getting my shield, she will
have to choose between getting her hair back and
saving that spidery friend of hers. Oh yes, that's
a much better deal.

A

MONDAY IO JULY

$$13:13$$

SHADEWELL ACADEMY, UNDER OUR TREE – BUT WITHOUT INNA

I've fresh determination for a fresh week at school – or, if all goes to plan, just one day. And then it's back through the well.

But it's not going all to plan. Not by a long shot.

I managed to escape my English lesson this morning, thinking I'd take the opportunity to race down to the basement and grab the shield. Maybe that's the way to do it?

NOPE.

I opened the staffroom door and came face to face with Ms Williams. So I have yet another detention for later, plus the head is now demanding to see my parent or carer. I have no idea what I can do about that. I'm certain Ms Williams won't want to see my recently turned human sea-monster sisters. So who?

But that's a problem for later. I've also made Inna cross. It turns out she is taking this inter-house school competition seriously – she actually cares about our class winning house points! So she is annoyed at me for repeatedly getting detentions and **LOSING** points. She somehow thinks winning the prize will mean she is making a success of her new life that her family sacrificed so much for. I said that it was **ONLY** a school competition.

"It's not just a school competition to me!"
she said, and then she walked off in a huff.
Maybe I shouldn't have said that.

18:18

HOME, BEDROOM

Yet another pupil in detention with us today.
It seems like every day there is someone new
to the school who's being sent to detention.
Maybe all new children struggle to settle in
and follow the rules. Apart from me, who is just
deliberately flouting them!

The new pupil today was a girl called **Echo.**

Apparently she'd been caught copying in a test. All she did for the entirety of detention was stare at Narcy — not that he noticed. Other than that, it was much the same as other days: Narcy was taking selfies; Dora was hugging her box; golden boy was wearing **even more** gold if such a thing were possible; and Talus was trying to eat the desk. Poor Mr Philson looked overwhelmed by the lot of us.

I still can't think what to do about the guardian problem. But hopefully Ms Williams will have forgotten about it tomorrow. And then we'll be out of here.

KOMOS

TUESDAY II JULY

12:59

SHADEWELL ACADEMY, UNDER OUR TREE – ALONE

It turns out Ms Williams has **NOT** forgotten that she requested a meeting with my guardian. She was waiting for me when I arrived at school this morning and has given me detention for later – and every day after that – until she actually sees my guardian. **BUM.**

No sign of Inna at our normal reading/writing place. I guess she's still annoyed. Hmmm. The news about my further detentions will **NOT** make her any happier with me.

$$\boxed{\textbf{20:01}}$$

HOME, KITCHEN

Have I just agreed to the **MOST RIDICULOUS SCHEME IN HISTORY?**

I think so. Yes.

My sisters have suggested that tomorrow, in order to stop my continued punishment from Ms Williams, **JEREMY** is going to go into school and pretend to be my guardian.

Yep. That's right. **THE MINOTAUR,** with his fairly limited vocabulary, will have a meeting with the head.

And why did I agree to this? Because Gail suggested that, while Ms Williams is distracted with her meeting, the rest of us can sneak into the basement and grab the shield.

We have to try it. I mean, what's the worst that could happen? I had tried to use detention to think of ways round this whole Ms Williams meeting problem, but I had come up with nothing, so I can't really complain about this absolutely ridiculous plan. I'd like to point out this wasn't my fault – there were lots of distractions during detention, so thinking clearly was quite tricky. Would you believe that yet another pupil joined our constantly growing group? And she was **NOT** happy about it. Cassie was supposed to be writing lines that said **"I must not lie"**, but instead she was shouting some really bizarre things.

"I have been sent here by a god to save me from my fate!" she howled.

The more she shouted, the less I believed her. Even though I have been sent here by ancient Greek gods, I simply did not believe a word she said.

The strangest thing is, I think I recognize this girl. But maybe I've just seen her around the school.

KOMOS

Look — and that new girl is clearly Cassandra! Come on. You have to believe me now.

Cassandra? I know about Cassandra. She was the Greek oracle known for being a BIG OLD LIAR!

Not exactly. She was cursed so that no one believed anything she said. Everyone thought she was a liar.

Well, it takes one to know one.

HA! Good one.

HOME, BEDROOM

It's late. I'm exhausted but I can't sleep. I've heard of people having restless legs when they can't sleep. I've got restless snakes. I really have no hope of this bizarre plan working tomorrow. It's not like I can get into MORE trouble, can I? What else can teachers in the twenty-first century do to punish a child? But for the sake of my friendship with Inna, I'd at least like to prevent further detentions. And, preferably, not be caught trying to pass off the Minotaur as my guardian, while my sisters and I essentially rob the school. That would not be the best thing. And maybe lose the inter-house competition in one fell swoop.

I did try to tell Arachne about the plan

earlier this evening, but something's not quite right with her. She just keeps weaving 'CONTRACT' and little dots. **WHAT IS SHE DOING?!**

Out of sheer desperation, while still at the well, I offered up a prayer to Aphrodite. If my years of adoration and worship – or the fact that I'm doing this to save my friend and her guardian – have been worth anything to the goddess of love then maybe, just maybe, she will hear my prayers and respond.

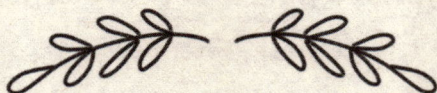

WEDNESDAY
12 JULY

$$\boxed{10:37}$$

SHADEWELL ACADEMY, GIRLS' TOILETS

OK, this morning has been **A LOT**. I'm writing this quickly at break time, so I get everything down in my diary.

The morning started off feeling positive. I had to admit that Jeremy looked quite dapper. My sisters had ordered him a suit from the **"Big Tall Man"** shop online, and it fitted him really well. The

top hat might have been overkill, but there was no other way to hide his horns. Looking at Jeremy, I started to believe this bonkers plan might **actually** work!

Jeremy and I arrived at school as planned. I was feeling very self-conscious, walking next to him, and my heart was pounding, but we made it. In fact, we'd passed the well and I saw a message from Arachne that read **"APHRODITE SENDING HELP"**, which made me feel really good. She'd answered my prayers, after all! It didn't even cross my mind to question this.

Ms Williams looked a bit startled when she came out of her office to meet us, as she took in Jeremy's height - and

APHRODITE SENDING HELP

hat – but she smiled, shook his massive hand and told me to wait outside. A few seconds later, my sisters ran through the doors (having disguised themselves as pupils and even removing their orange make-up and false eyelashes for the occasion), and we headed to the staffroom. It was empty – **A GOOD START!**

The plan was going to, well, plan.

And then it all went wrong.

Gail, Tina and I started down the steps into the

basement, but before we even reached the bottom, we heard a **SNARLING** and a **GROWLING** and a **BARKING** all at the same time. There, at the end of the corridor, was **CERBERUS** – Hades' **three-headed dog!** We pelted back up the steps and slammed the door behind us.

I was dangerously close to losing my temper about this new development, when a scream pierced the air.

I rushed out of the staffroom in the direction of the scream – the head's office.

Oh no! Had Jeremy **EATEN** Ms Williams?

I shoved open the door and was very relieved to find Ms Williams fully intact, albeit with all the colour drained from her face, looking like she'd seen a ghost. She was pointing at the open window and moving her mouth like a confused goldfish.

Jeremy helped explain the situation. **"Flying baby,"** he grunted.

Oh dear. That could only mean one thing – Aphrodite has sent **EROS**, the baby-sized god of love to help me!

Eros might look like a cute chubby baby, flying around with his downy wings and golden curls, but he is a foul-mouthed immortal troublemaker – and general toerag – who specializes in shooting people with his arrows to make them fall in love. In what **UNIVERSE** did Aphrodite think his presence here would help in any way, shape or form?

After spending about an hour chasing him around the school field with my sisters, we managed to grab him out of the air by one pudgy foot and wrestle him into my school bag. At least he's small! My sisters headed off back home to reapply their make-up and update their socials, and I headed back into school to assess the damage.

It is fair to say Eros is not happy about being in my bag. I can't even repeat the words that were coming out of his angelic little mouth, but this gives you the gist:

"Oi, you **XXXXXX**. I was sent by Aphrodite to

XXXXXX help you, you **XXXXXXX XXXXXXX**. And this is the **XXXXX** thanks I get? Let me out of this **XXXX** bag this instant. I'm going to **XXXX** out a whole nappy's worth of **XXXX** in here if you don't, you **XXXXXX**."

What a treasure!

With Eros secured as much as possible, I called back in to Ms Williams's office, only to find her perching on her desk right in front of a distressed-looking Jeremy, her hair loose and her glasses gripped between her teeth. She had Jeremy's tie between her fingers, and was alarmingly close to removing his top hat.

When he saw me, Jeremy grunted, **"Save me!"**

I gave my bag a strong shake, then opened it and demanded a lead arrow from Eros. Only one of his lead arrows can undo the love spell of a golden arrow.

"XXXXXX XXXXXX," came the delightful reply.

But with a few more rough shakes of my school bag Eros gave me what I'd requested.

As Ms Williams flicked her hair over a bemused Jeremy, I stabbed her with the tiny lead arrow. She uttered a small **"ow!"** and then immediately fell asleep on top of her desk, and Jeremy made his escape.

Hopefully, when Ms Williams wakes up, the lead arrow will have worked its magic to neutralize the gold one, and Ms Williams will no longer feel any love for Jeremy. And hopefully all she'll remember is meeting my guardian and *that* should put a stop to my endless detentions. At least I hope so!

As I left Ms Williams's office, Mr Philson was in the corridor.

"Is the head in?" he asked.

I told him she was busy, which should have been the end of it, if Eros hadn't decided to pipe up again with his high-pitched foul-mouthed tirade.

"**XXXXX** and **XXXXX**, you **XXXXXX**," Eros said. Very clearly.

Mr Philson whipped round. "What did you call me?" he demanded.

"Um, I think you know I called you a **XXXXX** and a **XXXXXX**," I repeated.

It is no surprise I have detention again after school.

$$13:15$$

SHADEWELL ACADEMY, GIRLS' TOILETS – AGAIN

It turns out it's quite exhausting wrestling a baby in a bag, which is what I've been doing since break time. You'd think it would be easy (not that I recommend it – babies should generally never be placed in bags), but when it comes to an immortal flying baby, it's trickier than you'd imagine. I kept Eros still and quiet under my desk during English by keeping my foot pressed down very **HARD** and very **THREATENINGLY** on the bag.

As soon as the bell went for lunch, I tried to race off to the well, to chuck my school bag down there, with Eros still in it. I didn't have long - and not because I'd miss my space in the lunch queue. No - Eros had worked out how to unzip my bag from the inside, so it was a battle to keep him securely bundled up. The only hope of getting him back through the well was to keep him **IN** the bag - otherwise I worried he could just fly back out. I'd almost made it to the school's front door, when I heard a **"Meddy!"**

I spun round to see Inna was following me.

"Everything OK?" she asked.

"I'm fine," I replied, trying to stop the bag from squirming.

"It's just that you weren't in first lesson, and

you looked ... stressed through English. Can I do anything?"

The bag unzipped itself and I quickly zipped it back up. Inna looked at the bag suspiciously but didn't ask any more questions.

I tried to smile but it was probably more of a grimace. "I'm fine. I've just got to deal with something quickly. Back in a tick."

I turned and pushed the door open, as Eros unzipped the bag yet again. Stupid baby. I ran through the front gates, up to the well, and threw the bag, complete with baby, into the well. As he is an immortal, I'm **almost** sure that Eros will be fine returning through the portal to ancient Greece, and won't implode or anything. **PROBABLY.**

HERMES EXPRESS
AIR TORTOISE (H.E.A.T.)
OFFICIAL CORRESPONDENCE BETWEEN
HADES AND ATHENA

H·E·A·T

Hades,

I've just heard from a most disgruntled Eros about his terrible treatment at the hands of Medusa. Skipping over the fact that he was in the twenty-first century at all (I will be having strong words with Aphrodite about that), just what does Eros mean when he says that Medusa appears to be in full health and even bonding well with her sea-monster sisters?

A

H·E·A·T

My dearest and most endearingly gullible Athena,
Oh, come on now. You can't believe the word of Eros! You know all he wants to do, as Aphrodite's playmate, is wind you up. Ignore him. Medusa is suffering plenty.

Hades

HOME – AND NO IDEA HOW TO LEAVE THE TWENTY-FIRST CENTURY

I returned home from detention today only to have to calm a **still-traumatized** Jeremy. (Ms Williams did reappear this afternoon – I saw her woozily meandering along the corridor – so I think that particular challenge has passed, even if the horror is still fresh in Jeremy's mind.) Detention barely registered with me this afternoon. I think I have to give up on the idea of ever getting the shield back to Athena. I might as well get used to the idea of being punished for all eternity, so why should an easy thing like detention bother me? My snakes aren't even disturbing me as I write. I'm no longer angry about this. **I. AM. JUST. TIRED.**

At each step, the gods have done things to

trip me up. Even when they're supposedly **trying** to help me, they make matters so much worse – thanks a lot, Aphrodite!

And what hope do I have of getting the shield with Cerberus guarding the basement? What hope is there that I can save myself and Arachne?

NONE!

I have only six days left and I am out of ideas. I might as well just stop trying.

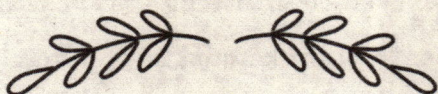

THURSDAY 13 JULY

22:12

HOME, BEDROOM

Today, for a change, I concentrated on being a twelve-year-old in school. What else can I do? I'm not about to fight the three-headed hound of the underworld, am I? So instead of plotting to get back the shield, I just focused on schoolwork. And it wasn't too bad! Apparently, if you're not trying to sneak out of class, or talking back to a teacher,

or wrestling a baby into a bag (obviously, not any baby, just Eros – I can't stress that enough), you get to learn stuff and teachers can be quite pleasant. I even got some house points today! Probably not enough to make Inna happy, but it made a refreshing change from losing them.

And today, for the first time in weeks – **NO DETENTION!**

I avoided Inna, though. I'd love to be her friend, but my time is running out here and so there's no real point to making things up with her. She came to find me at lunch and asked again if I was OK. I simply said, **"I'm fine."** She smiled sadly and walked away.

If I hadn't been sent to the twenty-first century on this mission, I might actually get to like it here. I still don't really know why Hades thinks it's torture here, but I've certainly had plenty of problems during my time in the twenty-first century. It's almost like I've been causing my own punishments.

This evening, with nothing to do for once, I spent more time at the well with Arachne. I almost felt like a normal twenty-first-century school pupil – other than the fact I was conversing with my spider best friend using a portal to ancient Greece. Arachne told me a few things, most of which were not news...

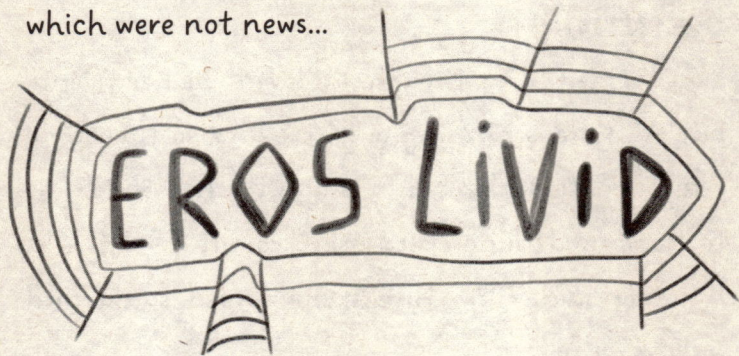

EROS LIVID

These words did not come as any surprise, and then she went back to weaving:

CONTRACT...

I wish she could tell me what she means. I don't want her to know that I am out of ideas about how to help her, but at some point I may have to confess that she'll be a spider forever, and that I'm failing her.

FRIDAY 14 JULY

10:32

SHADEWELL ACADEMY, GIRLS' TOILETS

It's Friday, which means it's collective worship day.
Thankfully the goat fiasco from the first week
has been forgotten (although I'm pleased to report
he's thriving on the shrubs in the garden – and,
occasionally, next door's washing). Ms Williams told
us about something called the French Revolution
in 1789, when the people of France rose up against

their tyrannical royal family and demanded their own rights and freedoms. Today marks the anniversary of that time. How brave those people must have been to stand up and fight. Liberty! Equality! Fraternity! **VIVE LA FRANCE!** Plus, Ms Williams also gave us all some delicious flaky pastries, which should be the way any collective worship session should end, in my opinion.

If only it was that easy in ancient Greece (fighting for power – not getting delicious pastries). How do you think the gods would deal with a revolution? Spiders and snake hair would be the least of anyone's troubles! Ah, still, I can dream!

13:15

SHADEWELL ACADEMY, UNDER OUR TREE

Inna is sitting with me this lunchtime. I didn't

ask her to. I was just minding my own business (and avoiding Sophie and the Os) when she sat down next to me.

She said, **"You know, sometimes it's OK not to be fine."**

I tried to insist that I **was** fine. I mean, other than the abject sense of failure and despair, I actually feel better and calmer than I have for my entire time here.

"I told you about my life, but you refuse to share anything about you," Inna said.

This was true. But what was I supposed to say? Hades' contract was clear that I couldn't tell anyone who I really am.

"Tell me a story, Meddy. Tell me anything. It doesn't have to be about you."

I sighed and puffed out my cheeks. Unable to think of anything better to talk about, I started telling her about my time in detention. I told her how sorry I felt for Dora, who was so obsessed with her box; how beautiful but vain I considered Narcy; how much in love Echo clearly was with Narcy; the boy with all the golden clothing; how I'd tried to help the starving Talus; and about the newest girl that lied all the time.

"Let me guess. That new girl is called Cassandra?" said Inna.

CASSIE? CASSANDRA! That was an impressive guess.

I felt better having told Inna **SOMETHING** about my experiences in school, even if it wasn't directly about me. But she went quiet and seemed to be deep in thought.

As the bell went for lessons, she just said, "Thanks for sharing that with me."

SATURDAY 15 JULY

```
10:30
```

HOME – FOR NOW

Oh no! This is it.

I'm about to be whisked back to ancient Greece without the shield, because someone knows who I am.

And that someone is Inna!

She called by our house this morning. I saw her from the small upstairs window. But between

my sisters' weird make-up, Jeremy and the goat, I
really didn't want her coming in, so I didn't even
open the door. I don't think it's how most people
live. And that's when she
called "Medusa!" through
the letter box. ———→

How does she know MY name? And if she knows
my real name, what other things might she know??

I wanted to ask her, but I can't give her an idea
that she's right. Even if she just suspects that's
who I am, it's probably already too late.

But what can I do? I can't hide in here forever.

16:22

HOME, BEDROOM

Inna returned again in the afternoon. This time
she didn't even ring the bell, but she simply posted

something through the door. It is the book she's always reading at lunchtime. With colourful bits of paper sticking out of different pages. The book is titled **The Myths of Ancient Greece**.

I took it to my bedroom to start reading and have barely looked up since.

I have no words.

I am hated.

I am despised.

I am notorious.

I am a monster.

I don't know where to start. I guess I just have to start at the beginning and hope for the best.

Sitting on my bed, I went to the first piece of coloured paper tucked in the pages, which was marked **Narcy and Echo?** It told the story of Echo and Narcissus: a girl made to fall so deeply in love with a boy, as punishment from a god, that she wasted away until nothing was left of her but her voice. The boy was then punished by a different god, and made to fall in love with his own reflection – until he could stand it no longer and died. Narcy and Echo? Those pupils from detention? Could they really be here in the twenty-first century?

I then moved on to another piece of paper (**Golden boy?**), marking the story of Midas – a king from ancient Greece who loved gold so much that he asked for the power to turn everything he touched into that precious metal. But he hadn't really thought it through, and so even the food he tried to eat turned to gold. Then there was a slip marked **Talus?**, telling the story of a boy named Tantalus, punished for ever in Tartarus and unable to take even the smallest sip of water or tiniest nibble of food. Echo? Narcissus? Midas? Tantalus?

As I read the story of Cassandra, the young oracle who had angered Apollo so much that he'd cursed her never to be believed, I suddenly remembered Cassandra back in ancient Greece. I'd laughed at her ridiculous lies. I remember scoffing at her prophecy about being known throughout history for my terrible hair. Well, I'm no longer laughing. Could that be the same girl that is here in Shadewell now? No wonder I didn't believe what she was shouting about in detention. What is she doing in the twenty-first century? Why are ANY of these mortals here?

I flicked to the page about Pandora. Not Dora. **Pandora**. She was the first female, created by Zeus as a way of punishing all humankind when Prometheus shared the gift of fire. Everyone in the temple knew the story of Pandora – she was always held up as an example of the cruelty of the gods. She was tasked by Zeus to look after a box and told NEVER to look in it. Was it her fault that curiosity got the better of her?

There was one piece of paper remaining,

marking the page for **Medusa?** I couldn't bring myself to look at it, so I flicked to other pages, finding the story of Actaeon, punished by Artemis. Of Daphne, chased by Apollo until she prayed to the gods to be killed. Of the nameless Minotaur – a monster kept in a labyrinth in order to torment others. I thought of gentle Jeremy, still shaken by his experience with Eros and Ms Williams. There was no mention of his kind soul in Inna's book.

I also found the story of my best friend Arachne, punished by Athena for being too good at embroidery. There was no mention of my name in Arachne's story. Did that mean that Arachne's punishment would have happened whether I was there or not? Or perhaps it was just a detail that had been lost to history.

Story after story, page after page, were tales of humans being tricked and chased and attacked by sly, selfish, self-serving gods.

I took as deep a breath as possible, swallowing the bile that was rising in my throat, and turned to the final page that Inna had marked. This is what it said:

Medusa Gorgon and her sea-monster sisters, Euryale and Stheno, are among the most reviled creatures from ancient Greece. After being attacked by Poseidon in Athena's temple, Medusa was punished by the goddess of war and wisdom with a head of hideous snakes and a face so grotesque that anyone who looked upon her immediately turned to stone. Her monstrous life was finally ended by one of the greatest heroes of all time, Perseus. This young man received assistance from various gods in his righteous quest and was able to kill the vile Medusa by chopping off her head. Once dead, the winged horse Pegasus sprang from Medusa's blood.

Monstrous?

Grotesque?

Turning people to stone?

Is that my story? Is that my **fate**?

I'm just...

I can't.

KOMOS

With Medusa so distraught, it really doesn't feel like the time to say "**I told you so.**" But didn't I tell you that other ancient Greek mortals were turning up in Medusa's story?

Yeah, yeah. No one likes a smarty-pants.

22:15

HOME, IN BED

This day just gets worse and worse. You'd think it would be enough to be reeling from the information I read in Inna's book - just how are you supposed to deal with the news that you're an infamous monster who turns people to stone? - but now I've also discovered that my sisters are back-stabbing monsters.

After reading ... **that**, I took myself to bed. I didn't want to face anything.

Not my sisters. Not the world. Nothing.

But Gail and Tina came into my room a while ago. They'd brought some food, which is still uneaten by my bed, and they tried to make me feel better. I wanted to show them our story, but they didn't want to see it. They

didn't want to know their fate.

And the reason?

Because they're **BACK-STABBING MONSTERS**. **That's** the reason.

I knew something was up when Tina and Gail started giving each other strange looks. At first, I thought one of Tina's false eyelashes was bothering her, but it turned out they were signalling to each other to confess about **BEING BACK-STABBING MONSTERS**.

Have I mentioned they're back-stabbing monsters? I feel I cannot emphasize that enough.

After a bit of "You tell her", "No, you tell her" back and forth, Gail cleared her throat and said, "We've got something we need to tell you. We're not going back to ancient Greece."

"So it doesn't matter what a silly old book says about us," added Tina. "We're changing our fate."

"But you're here as my carers. It was all part

of the contract. We're supposed to get the shield and all return together," I said.

"Well, Hades offered us this option, and it sounded better than living in a cave," said Gail.

"Hades?" At the mention of his name, my stomach lurched. "Hades never does anything just for the sake of others. What did he get you to do?"

Both my sisters looked uncomfortable. They shuffled around and refused to meet my gaze.

"TELL ME!" I said.

"We just had to delay you getting to the shield too quickly. Hades wanted us to make sure you stayed here for as long as possible," said Gail.

I'd thought my sisters were on my side. That they were helping me. But they were only helping themselves. My heart started thumping. No wonder they didn't turn up on the evening I planned to steal the shield.

"Please try to stay **calm**," Tina said. "You mustn't lose your temper. What about the snakes?"

"As if you care," I snapped. "You've been making me fail at each turn. Why should I even bother to try any more?"

"**NO!** Please believe us. We were only doing things that would **delay** your task. Hades doesn't want you to fail. He said he just needed the time."

"Time to torture me!" I yelled. "So it was **YOU** who told the police about the planned break-in. It was **YOU** who asked Hades to send Jeremy. You disappeared for days. All in the name of delaying me getting to the shield. All at the risk of making me fail! Don't you even care that I'll be stuck with snake hair for ever? And what about poor Arachne?"

Thinking about Arachne was the final straw. My scalp started prickling and my vision blurred. I was either going to faint, vomit or be rushed back to ancient Greece with a head full of snakes – or all three. But, at that moment, Mr Car and Ian appeared in front of my face, fixing me with hypnotic stares. They swayed gently and hissed in long calming breaths. Were they trying to ... **help me?**

While I was transfixed by their eyes, my sisters continued talking, trying to justify their underhand actions. Hades had given them the chance to escape from their lives as cave-dwelling sea monsters, could I not understand that? Well, suddenly lots of things made sense. It certainly explained why they were so keen to learn everything about this time as soon as we arrived. No wonder they wanted to make jobs and lives for themselves. They never intended to return to ancient Greece.

My breathing slowed and I allowed myself to turn my gaze from Mr Car and Ian. The danger of completely losing it had passed. But – the **BETRAYAL!**

OK, so I can see why my sisters wouldn't want

to go back to being sea monsters, but they are still **BACK-STABBING MONSTERS**. Although I can't blame them really, I suppose. But I **CAN** blame their puppet master Hades, that appalling sneaky god of the dead.

Not that any of this matters anyway. Once the gods find out that someone knows who I am, my mission is over. And it'll be back to ancient Greece for a life of...

My snakes are now barely reacting to any of this as I write.

I am numb.

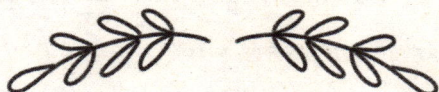

SUNDAY 16 JULY

09:21

HOME, THE LIVING ROOM

I had been intending to spend all day – and probably the rest of my time here – in bed, hiding from the world and from my future. You know the one: where I'm punished for all time by being transformed into a hideous snake-haired monster who turns anyone who looks at them to stone. But lying there, feeling sorry for myself, there was one niggling thought that kept repeating in my mind – what about Arachne?

My life is pretty much doomed and I doubt I can do anything about that, but if there is a chance of saving my friend, I have to try it.

Ha! Even that – even my desire to **TRY** to save my friend, when the chances are so slim – is the work of the gods. The gods know how to mess with us at every stage. That box that Zeus gave to Pandora? When Pandora opened it, she unleashed sickness, war and death. But there was one thing remaining at the bottom of the box: **HOPE**.

It is **HOPE** that keeps us going. And if I am still here, there is still a chance I can save my friend. Hope, that **"gift"** from the gods, will make me keep going. Perhaps it is the cruellest thing of all.

To borrow a phrase from Eros, the gods can just **"XXX XX"**.

HOME, KITCHEN

So more of Hades' trickery and deception comes to light.

I KNEW IT! I knew sneaky Hades would find a way to mess up my mission. No wonder he was so keen to **"help out"** by giving me permission to come here.

I have finally discovered what Arachne means when she's been weaving **"CONTRACT"** and those dots. I went to talk to her through the well, telling her everything that has been happening – everything I now know – and she just kept responding with **"CONTRACT"**. She wasn't being taken over by weird spideryness – no, she had spotted something.

CONTRACT...

Maybe having eight eyes **IS** useful.

It seemed like a pointless task at first. I found my copy of the contract, but there was nothing else to it. No decorations, no fancy flourishes. Nothing that I hadn't seen before. But Arachne had been weaving **"CONTRACT"** for days – and lots of dots. And that's when I saw them! There were extra full stops to some of the rules!

NUMBER SEVEN: No other humans or creatures from ancient Greece will be able to enter the twenty-first century.

NUMBER EIGHT: Ways for Medusa to fail in the mission include but are not limited to:
- She runs out of time.
- She tells someone who she is.
- She doesn't keep her temper and breaks Athena's masking spell ☺

NUMBER NINE: If Medusa fails in this task, she will be immediately returned to Athena's temple at the base of Mount Olympus. Athena will be permitted to continue her planned punishment of Medusa and Arachne will remain a spider.☺

Something easy to miss – or easy to put down to poor editing. **BUT NO!** I do not possess spider eyes (snake hair is bad enough), **BUT** I do possess sisters with phones with cameras, sisters who feel very sorry about being back-stabbing monsters, so who are trying to be nice and helpful.

They scanned the contract and zoomed in on those extra dots – and there is **WRITING THERE!**

So Rule Seven actually reads:

No other humans or creatures from ancient Greece will be able to enter the twenty-first century *after Medusa's mission has ended or the portal has been destroyed.*

So no wonder other mortals and creatures have been coming through! Hades has been having his fun while I've been suffering here.

Rule Eight reads:

Ways for Medusa to fail in the mission include but are not limited to: She doesn't keep her temper and breaks Athena's masking spell, *in which case the contract will be broken and the portal destroyed.*

Hmmm. I don't really know why this was hidden in the contract. Hades is up to some kind of trickery, of course.

And Rule Nine reads:

If Medusa fails in this task, she will be immediately returned to Athena's temple at the base of Mount Olympus. Athena will be permitted to continue her planned punishment of Medusa and Arachne will remain a spider, *unless Medusa succeeds in returning the shield but chooses to stay in the twenty-first century.*

Chooses to stay in the twenty-first century?
What's that about? Since when do I have any
kind of choice about anything? And why hide
that from me?

I would say that I can't believe that Hades
hid extra details in the contract but, actually,
I can fully believe it of that scheming, devious
stinky-egg god.

My head is spinning. Why has Hades done
any of this?

I think I understand why he hid the detail for
Rule Seven - he wanted Athena to think that other
creatures couldn't enter the portal, while giving him
the chance to send whatever he wanted: Jeremy,
Cerberus and who knows what else!

So not only did he trick me into signing
something I didn't fully understand, but
he also tricked Athena. **ALWAYS READ THE
SMALL PRINT** - it's the first rule of contract

signing. The problem is, I wasn't even aware there **was** any small print. I should have trusted my gut from the start and never agreed to this

TERRIBLE

mission. I was never going to escape my punishment or my fate.

I'm not feeling very hopeful any more. I'm going back to bed.

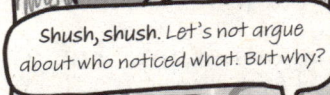

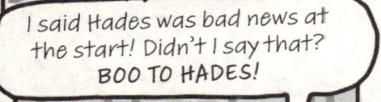

HOME, BEDROOM

Lying in bed, **thinking** about your problems, is apparently not the best way of dealing with them. I was trying to keep my mind blank and simply wait for further punishment, but it hasn't happened yet.

Maybe I haven't yet been summoned back to Athena, even though Inna knows who I am, because the contract says I cannot TELL anyone who I am. Well, I have not done that. Inna just guessed. Perhaps that's why I'm still here?

While I've been lying here, all kinds of different thoughts have been nagging at me.

Here are some of them:

- So Hades has been using my time here to send other ancient Greek mortals through the portal. That much is clear. But I have no idea why.
- For some reason, he's written into the contract a way for me to stay in the twenty-first century. If I get the shield to Athena, I can choose to stay. Why would I do that?
- And if I break Athena's masking spell by losing my temper, that will destroy the portal.

But that's not all. I gave the contract another read and noticed something I missed before:

Should the mortal known as Medusa Gorgon succeed in retrieving the shield, Athena, goddess of war, wisdom and handicrafts, does hereby agree to end all ~~future~~ current punishments of Medusa (OR) to turn the mortal known as Arachne back to human form.

When I signed this contract, I'm sure it said **"AND"**, not **"OR"**. When did that change? Another example of the gods' treachery.

Whatever I do, I'm not going to win. But I don't care about what happens to me or my stupid hair any more; I just want to save my friend. I need to get Athena's shield back through the well so at least Arachne can be saved, but I don't think I'm even able to do that. With Cerberus guarding the shield and time running out, I just can't see a way to help Arachne now.

16:51

HOME, BEDROOM

I've changed my mind - THERE IS ALWAYS HOPE!

Inna came back round this afternoon and

this time I let her in.

I wasn't sure how much I could say to her, without it counting as "telling" her who I was, so I tried to let her **happen** to see various things. She **MAY** have seen Jeremy sitting in the living room, taking up most of the space with his huge bulk. She **MAY** have caught a glimpse of Mr Car and Ian as I ran my fingers through my hair. And she **MAY** also have seen the contract that just happened to be lying on the kitchen table. She may have spent a few minutes reading that contract. I told her nothing.

After Inna had taken in the small print, she looked at me and asked, "So what are you going to do?"

I shrugged.

"You can't be considering going back to ancient Greece, can you?"

I ran my hand across the table, hoping it looked like a spider – this was all for Arachne.

"Can't she come through the portal? It sounds like plenty of others have made that journey."

The thought had crossed my mind too, but if she did that, how would Athena's curse on her ever be broken? Surely Arachne needs to still be in ancient Greece when I return the shield through the portal so that she can be returned to being human.

"Perhaps it's a choice you need to give her?" Inna suggested. And then she went on: "I know about making tough choices. My family had to make a tough choice to come here. But sometimes you have to understand that you're not going to change anything by staying in a place that means danger and death, even if that place used to be your home. You know what your fate will be if you return. But you don't have to accept that."

Inna got up to leave, but turned and said, "Whatever you decide, I can try to help," and she placed something on the table.

It was a tiny gold arrow – Eros's arrow. How did she get hold of that?

There is always hope – and I now have a new plan!

I can deal with Cerberus and I can get the shield!

19:06

HOME, AND COUNTING DOWN TO NIGHTFALL

I am just back from updating Arachne about discovering our stories and learning that other ancient Greek mortals are here in the twenty-first century, and about my new plan to retrieve the shield.

Turns out Inna is sneakier than I gave her credit for. She took Eros's arrow when he was having a nap in class. Now that I have it, I know I can get the shield and save her. I don't know if the gods thought I would be in a terrible quandary over whether to save myself or my best friend, but there is no real choice. Of course I'm going to save my best friend.

I didn't actually tell her about the change from **"AND"** to **"OR"** in the contract. She doesn't need to know that it can't be both of us that will be saved when the shield is back with Athena. I hope she hasn't noticed herself. I did tell her that I'd found the hidden details in the contract. I thought she'd be pleased but I didn't get a response. Maybe she's asleep? Do spiders sleep?

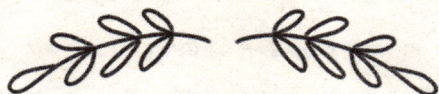

MONDAY 17 JULY

02:11

HOME, KITCHEN

Why is nothing here ever straightforward?

The first part of my plan went beautifully: in the dead of night my duplicitous sisters, Jeremy and I entered the school. Armed with mirrors, we made our way down to the basement. As Cerberus charged at us, Jeremy used Eros's tiny golden arrow to stab the snarling creature. And all three heads were suddenly and utterly entranced by their own reflections – Cerberus had fallen in love with himself! **(I have to thank Inna's book and the story of Narcissus for this idea.)**

With Cerberus now focused on the mirrors, we were able to coax him out of the basement and towards the well. We dropped the mirrors down the well, and Cerberus leaped in after them.

That left the way clear to get back to the basement, retrieve the shield and enter the well. Success was so close I could almost taste it.

And then it wasn't.

I rushed through the basement with Jeremy by my side **(far better than him chasing me),** ready to retrieve the shield, only to find that the final door of the basement – the one

to the room holding Athena's shield – was secured by a massive lock. Even Jeremy, with his rippling muscles, was unable to break through it. This is completely my sisters' fault. If they hadn't called the police in the first place, the shield wouldn't be secured away down here.

Now there is no way I can get my hands on the shield.

Except...

The inter-house school competition!

┌─────────────┐
│   **12:35**   │
└─────────────┘

SHADEWELL ACADEMY,
UNDER OUR TREE

This feels like I'm cutting things horribly close. Tomorrow is the last day of my allotted time here, the last day of term **and** the day when the winning house will be announced for the inter-house school competition. Miss Morley's eyebrows jumped towards her hairline when I showed an interest in the scores.

"Austen House is **NECK-AND-NECK** with Zephaniah House, so it's all down to these last two days," she said. "But as long as **no one** gets detention, there is hope!"

YES! There **IS** always hope.

Clearly, the school takes the competition and the prize-giving very seriously. Outside the front entrance of the school, a temporary stage is being built. It seems ambitious to organize an **OUTSIDE** event in this cold wet country, but, seeing Ms Williams arranging seating within sight of the well, a new plan is forming in my mind.

I'm currently sitting with Inna, but it's difficult to give her any details of my plan for fear of accidentally "telling" her anything about me. I hope she will understand what I have to do next. I hope she will trust me, because I do intend to help Austen House win the inter-house school competition – not just for my mission but also for her. But first I have to get a detention!

17:10

HOME, BEDROOM

Inna is a great friend. I'm going to miss her when I return to ancient Greece tomorrow...

It turns out it's really difficult to get detention when you're actively trying. Everyone is in an end-of-term good mood, so my rudeness was just laughed away by Miss Carlton in art class. Even Mr Philson barely took any notice of me. Then I thought about Sophie! Sophie was an all-teachers' favourite, and she wasn't going to let any kind of insult go. If **she** complained about me, that would be different. So I told her that she **swished her hair like a horse's bottom** - and THAT got me detention. PERFECT!

HORSE'S BOTTOM

But in detention I started to panic. Mr Philson was standing at the front, glowering at me, and my time to talk to the other pupils was running out. Not only that but I also hadn't actually thought of what I'd say to everyone - and, of course, I couldn't **TELL** them who I am!

I was almost losing hope as the minutes ticked away, but then the door opened and there was Inna.

"Mr Philson, Ms Williams needs to see you in,

erm, the sports hall," she said.

Inna had bought me some time! She'd managed to send the teacher to the furthest away part of the school on a wild goose chase. And not only that but Inna also spoke to all the ancient Greek mortals for me. She'd brought her book with her, so she was able to show Narcissus, Midas and the others their stories and their fates. It turns out they each knew they'd been transferred from ancient Greece to a new time and **(very cold)** place but they were not aware that there were others. Inna was amazing – she explained who I was and then passed over to me with just enough time for me to share the basic idea of tomorrow's plan, and everyone's roles in it, before Mr Philson returned, looking out of breath and very annoyed. Hopefully, these ancient Greeks will help me get the shield and myself through the portal to save my friend.

HOME – WITH MY BEST FRIEND!

Arachne is here! Arachne is in the twenty-first century! She's ruined my plan to save her. My plan for tomorrow was going to work – but she's gone and jumped through the portal.

I'd gone to tell her not to lose hope and that, even though it's really last-minute, my new plan to get the shield will almost certainly work. But when I got to the well, there was a new web message, which said 'I here', and she was sitting on her web, alongside her message.

I was so pleased to see her that I picked her up and tried to hug her, but hugging a spider is tricky and I didn't want Mr Car or Ian to eat her.

Then, after a whispered apology, I tried to throw her back into the well – according to the

contract, she needs to be in ancient Greece when I return the shield tomorrow, or she'll stay as a spider forever. But she grabbed firm to my fingers. Then she weaved the messages **"AND/OR"** and **"MY CHOICE"**.

So Arachne **had** seen the change to the contract. And she's chosen to jump through the portal and risk remaining a spider? Surely flies can't be *that* delicious?!

I was ready with a plan to save my best friend, but she has chosen to change her fate.

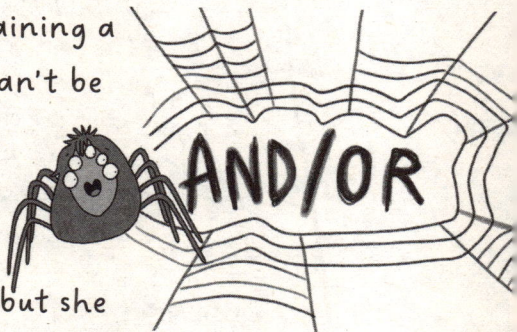

Where, exactly, does that leave me?

HERMES EXPRESS
AIR TORTOISE (H.E.A.T.)
OFFICIAL CORRESPONDENCE BETWEEN
HADES AND ATHENA

Hades,

Enough of this! There's no sign of my shield coming back to me from Medusa herself. I can't wait for you to return her to me, so I can get started on her punishment properly. I don't know why I agreed to this nonsense in the first place. Of course she was going to fail. She's a worthless human. But when she fails, you WILL bring me my shield, right?

A

My dearest and most
fabulously astute Athena,

Aren't all humans worthless,
really? But hasn't it been fun to
mess with Medusa? The challenges
I created for her here have just
been too tough. Still, you only had to
wait an extra twenty-four days, and
what's that to an immortal? If
Medusa fails, of course I will bring
the shield to you. It's in the contract,
so you know I will.

Hades

END OF ACT 2

ACT 3

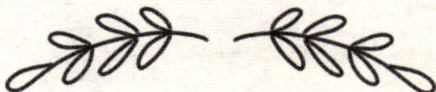

TUESDAY 18 JULY

06:10

HOME, BEDROOM

I woke up really early this morning, feeling **UTTERLY SICK**. I thought it was nerves. My stomach is churning and my palms feel clammy – but then I became aware of laughter coming from downstairs. And a very particular smell.

The smell of rotten eggs.

HADES!

I rushed downstairs, ready to – I don't know what. What can you do to an immortal?

He was sitting with my sisters, who were serving him a cup of tea! **TEA!**

I should have expected that. After all, they had a deal with him.

Jeremy was also with him, and there, on the table, was Arachne.

He beamed. "Ah, here is the girl of the hour! You know, I really have been *very* impressed with you. I haven't known another human try so hard with one of my challenges. And you've nearly done it. You've kept your temper. You're so close to the shield. The question now is: what are you going to do with the shield once you get hold of it?"

Seeing him sitting there, so smug, made me want to ~~grab at his hair~~ and ... **10, 9, 8, 7, 6, 5, 4, 3, 2, 1**. He sensed my mood and quickly added, "You really don't want to lose your temper with me now, do you? That really would ruin everything you've been working for."

I took some deep breaths but gagged on the rotten-egg smell.

Holding back vomit, I said, "I'm going to get that shield, return to ancient Greece, tell Athena what you've been up to and hope that information is enough to get her to lift the curse on Arachne."

"But Arachne is here now. She's made her choice – and, as far as I can tell, she's happy as a spider. How do you know if a spider is happy? Well, never mind that. What about YOU, Medusa? Athena is a powerful enemy to have. And you now know what your future holds if you return to ancient Greece. Do you think you can really escape your fate if you go back?"

I looked at Hades, trying to work out exactly what he was playing at. "I know you've been using me to bring other ancient Greeks here," I said. "You're so used to dealing with the dead that you have no feelings. No empathy. I've heard you speak about us when you've been hanging around the temples at the base of Mount Olympus. All the gods are bad – but surely you are the worst."

I waited to be struck down, but, instead, Hades

gave me a little clap and rose from his chair. **"Perfect. Perfect!"** he exclaimed. "That's exactly what I need you to think. You see, as god of the underworld, yes, I deal with the dead of all kinds: those who have led the best lives and those who have done terrible things. I've seen humans in all times and places. I know humans far better than any of the gods who just stay up at the top of Mount Olympus. I know people can't always be blamed for their actions. And I know that many of them will redeem themselves given half a chance."

"Then why are you so horrible?"

"Am I? I seem to remember that I saved your life and persuaded Athena to let you come here."

"To torture me!" I said.

"Oh no, no, no. I had to make Athena think that was what was happening to you, so she'd agree to the plan! While you've been in the twenty-first century, I've been busy putting Athena off

the scent. I've spent millennia trying to help lots of humans, but particularly those who were destined for awful punishments from the gods. Unfortunately, Zeus got wise to me interfering and stopped me from meddling directly; he's even stopped me from being able to enter my own portal. My own portal! Now I can only enter with specific permission from another god! So I have to rely on tricks. I tricked Athena into granting permission for you to come here, by giving her what she wants. You were the key to all of this. Once Athena had granted permission for you and your sisters to travel through my portal, and with that bit of sneakiness you found in the contract, I also arranged it so I could save other Grecians—"

"And TERRIFY me with the likes of Cerberus!" I said.

"You were safe from Old Softie. That was only to delay you finishing the mission and

ending the contract too soon. You being here created a link to the twenty-first century that could be used to bring others here, for as long as your mission lasted. I did try to make your contract last five hundred years, but Athena put a stop to that. Still, thanks to you – and the delaying tactics of your sisters, of course – plenty will no longer suffer their fates."

I stared at him. "But why me?"

"It could have been anyone, really. I placed my well in the temple complex and started the row between Athena and Aphrodite – and when you sow that kind of chaos, there will always be some kind of fallout. And when gods aren't happy, it will always be a human who suffers – and *that* human will be willing to take a deal. Bish bash bosh. Gods agree to punishment and grant permission, contract signed, portal linked up – job done. And Zeus is none the wiser. It's a careful balancing act. I have a certain ... reputation to uphold. To answer your question: you threw Athena's shield in the well. I saw the opportunity to put my plan into action and took it."

"So ... you're **helping** people?"

"Shhhh. Don't go spreading it around!"

Could this really be true? Hades, most hated and hideous god of the dead, actually *saving* people? Or was this another of his tricks?

"Look, I know this has been hard on you, but thanks to you many humans have escaped their fate. We've saved them." Hades smiled. Then his smile turned to a frown as he continued, "But Athena's about as powerful a nemesis as you can get, Medusa. I had to make this challenge really difficult to keep her playing along. I could just grab the shield and return with it to ancient Greece, but then you will be recalled to face Athena, as per the contract. You would be punished forever. The only good thing about that plan is certainty. I don't know whether Arachne will be returned too – I'm a bit unclear on that as I didn't expect her to jump if I'm honest."

"Maybe I'll get the shield back to Athena myself and tell her exactly what you've been up to. Surely she'll treat me favourably after that? Then she'll help both me and Arachne," I said.

"You know exactly what punishment Athena will dish out. Even if you please her for now, you know what your fate will be. Do you want to turn people to stone? **REALLY?** Here, now, you have a chance to change that. So you have a choice to make: either you let me take the shield back now and admit defeat, or you use what is written in the contract and change your fate. I can't help you any more than that – I am risking any future aid I might be able to give humans as it is just by being here."

My mind wandered back to the contract. Is this what Hades had planned all along? Giving me a way out of returning to ancient Greece and being punished for all time by Athena? Is **THAT** what the small print meant? Somehow, if I return the shield to Athena but also destroy the portal, I could be safe? Was that true? Could I trust Hades?

His voice broke through my thoughts. "What is it to be? Should I take the shield with me?"

"NO!" my sisters shouted.

So by the time my final day of school starts, in just a couple of hours, I need to have come up with a new plan that allows me to return the shield and somehow remain here in the twenty-first century. If Hades is to be believed (which much of me still doubts), the contract is the key to working this problem out.

The small print does mention a way of

destroying the portal. Does that mean...? **Will I have to...?**

Oh no! I think I'm about to have a **VERY** bad hair day.

KOMOS

10:33

SHADEWELL ACADEMY, GIRLS' TOILET – HOPEFULLY FOR THE VERY LAST TIME!

Right. The first part of my plan is in place! I have just secured the inter-house school prize for Austen House – yay me! **WHOOP WHOOP!** – and how did I manage this particular feat? Well, I remembered Miss Morley asking us to bring in work done at home – so I did! There is something I've been working on the entire time I've been here in the twenty-first century – this diary! By the time I arrived at school, I had copied out some choice extracts from the diary and I handed them in to Ms Williams **(I made sure to remove any reference to Eros and Jeremy!).** For my hard work, and for going "above and beyond with my imaginative diary-style piece of writing",

Ms Williams awarded me five house points, which Miss Morley was delighted to announce to our tutor group. No one really seemed that interested that our house had won the inter-house competition apart from Inna, but that's all I cared about! I felt proud, until Sophie pointed out that I'd actually lost the class more points than that by constantly being put in detention. Still, a win is a win, right?

Not only have we won the shield, but as the child responsible for getting those final crucial points for Austen House, I have been given the honour of collecting the shield.

YES!

This brings me to the second part of my plan. I just have to make sure everyone is in position when the prize-giving starts this afternoon. If that goes wrong, this may be the last time I write in this. So wish me luck, dear Diary. **Laters!**

HERMES EXPRESS
AIR TORTOISE (H.E.A.T.)
OFFICIAL CORRESPONDENCE BETWEEN
HADES AND ATHENA

Hades,

Thanks for the shield. I rather like its new golden look. As Medusa did not return with it, I assume she failed in her task. Please bring her to me so I can continue punishing her.

Athena

My dearest and most marvellously merciful Athena,

I am pleased you are happily in possession of your beloved shield. But you should know that, in the end, I was not the one to return it. Medusa did indeed succeed in sending the shield through the portal, but tragically lost her temper at the last moment, so the portal was destroyed and she is now trapped in the twenty-first century. I don't think I'm able to get her back for you now the contract is finished. But technically she did succeed, so you no longer need to punish her, do you? And what a delightful twist – Medusa will now be stuck for all time being horribly punished in the worst place I've ever known.

Hades

Hades,

Is it REALLY that bad there?

A

H.E.A.T

My dearest, dearest, dearest Athena,

A secondary school in the twenty-first century? It's ABSOLUTE TORTURE!

Hades

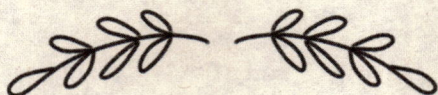

TUESDAY 18 JULY

15:50

Dear Diary,

I am still here!

It worked. My plan worked. I am so relieved.

The challenge is over. Athena's shield has been returned through the portal, and the portal has been destroyed.

And, best news of all, Arachne is human again!

HUMAN
ARACHNE!

THE END!

Oh, go on then. I'll share the details.

I can't take all the credit for this. It turns out I do like groups of people when they're MY people – and my people just happen to be quirky misfits: Arachne (whether in human or spider form!), Inna, my sisters, Jeremy and the other humans sent from ancient Greece. Inna was really helpful in getting the other ancient Greek mortals on board with the last-minute NEW plan – and telling them that if it works, we (Inna, my sisters, Jeremy and I) will help them to settle in better to this new time and learn to free themselves from their fates. They can't all be stuck in detention forever. And, on the whole, everyone followed their parts beautifully.

So what exactly happened? Well, for a while I did think no one would actually survive the prize-giving ceremony. It was so boring! But one by one, the awards were handed out and the draped table became a bit emptier. Finally only the huge inter-house school prize – Athena's shield – remained. Seeing the shield glinting there, but trying not to just grab it, was TORTURE.

Ms Williams picked it up, straining under its weight, and announced the winning house.

"This prize will be collected by one of our newer pupils, who, I think it is fair to say, has struggled to settle since arriving," said Ms Williams into a black stick (I have since learnt it is called a microphone), "but she has really demonstrated school spirit and shown that, given the chance, any pupil can turn things round. And, to my complete surprise, she has offered to do a little speech as part of this ceremony. Meddy Gordon, please come up."

Ms Williams handed me the shield. It sparkled in the sunshine and the metal was warm to the touch. I staggered with the weight of it. The head moved to allow me to speak into the microphone and this was when the next stage of my plan started.

"Erm, hello, everyone. Actually, Cassandra is going to speak for me," I said.

Cassandra joined me on the stage. Ms Williams looked a bit surprised but did not complain.

Cassandra moved towards the microphone.

This was it.

I walked to the edge of the stage and handed the shield to Echo, who was waiting there as planned.

"Meddy has handed the shield to Echo," said Cassandra.

Echo moved through the audience and handed the shield to Narcissus.

"Echo has handed the shield to Narcissus."

The audience started to look confused. Excellent. This was exactly what I wanted. Cassandra was telling the audience precisely what was happening. They could even SEE what was happening with their own eyes. But because of Cassandra's curse, no one could believe what she was saying! It was perfect.

"Narcissus is staring at his reflection in the shield."

Oh dear, I should have realized that would be an issue. Thankfully Midas came to the rescue. As soon as he touched the shield, it turned from silver to gold.

"Midas has grabbed the shield from Narcissus."

No one from the audience was trying to get the shield back. No one was moving at all. We were stealing the shield right in front of everyone, but thanks to the cursed Cassandra describing the action, no one believed it!!

"Now Midas has passed the shield to Tantalus."

Gail was waiting on the other side of the closed school gate, ready for Tantalus to pass the shield to her and Tina.

"And Tantalus has squeezed through the closed gate. Goodness, he is skinny. Someone give that boy a decent meal!"

This was not part of the plan. But still the shield was heading towards the well.

"Tantalus has dodged Tina. Now he has pushed a big man in a top hat. Now he is climbing on to the well. Now he has jumped into the well and disappeared, along with the shield.

And that's it! The end."

So Tantalus decided to return to ancient Greece? No problem. I guess he didn't like the idea of staying in the twenty-first century. It does take some getting used to. At least the shield had entered the portal – that was what mattered.

And now, it was time for the final part of my plan: destroying the portal!

The small print was quite clear – if I **told** anyone who I was, I would be whisked back through the portal. There was still a risk that could happen at any second. **BUT** Hades had given me a way to destroy the portal once and for all: **I had to lose my temper.**

I stood in front of the whole school, willing my snakes to appear. I had spent so much of the last twenty-four days – of my life, even – trying to control my anger but now, when I needed to let loose, nothing was happening. What was going on?

I tried to muster feelings of self-pity and kick-start my anger that way. After all, I'd been unfairly punished and sent to a strange time and place by a vengeful goddess. But, as I looked to my sisters, still standing outside the school railings, they waved and cheered, and warmth flooded over me. Spending time with them had actually been a good thing. I looked round at the other ancient Greeks, all here because of me (and Hades' trickery); they'd just helped me complete my task. Even looking at Sophie and the Os made me thankful that I'd managed to escape their group and find a proper friend in Inna.

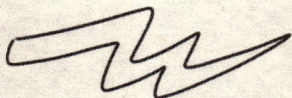

I must have looked quite silly, just standing there in front of the microphone, smiling goofily.

The audience started to fidget.

"Get on with it, Fart Face," shouted Oscar.

Even this didn't rile me.

But this wasn't the plan. I looked over at the portal - if I didn't do something quickly to destroy it, would Athena summon me back? Time was running out.

I focused on the microphone. But I couldn't think of what to say without **TELLING** everyone who I really was.

Just at that moment, the black foam ball at the top of the microphone started to move. I blinked and looked harder. It took a couple of seconds for my eyes to adjust, but there, barely discernible from the microphone itself, was Arachne!

Arachne - my best friend. My poor

spidery friend, who only ever saw the good in me, and who'd started off my diary-writing journey. Arachne, whose amazing talent should be a cause for celebration, not punishment. Arachne, who had jumped through the portal to stop me having to choose whether to save her or myself.

How could Athena have punished this poor human? All Arachne had ever done was admire Athena and try to be as good at embroidery as her. And for that, here she was – **A SPIDER.**

The more I focused on the unfairness of Arachne's situation, the more my scalp prickled. **My hair started to stand on end.**

With one hand, I carefully picked up Arachne and held her aloft, so the audience could see her. With the other, I unpinned my hair, shaking it loose so that Mr Car and Ian would become visible. I heard them hiss over my shoulders.

The audience gasped. Suddenly the image of Athena reaching out with her invisible touch, her face contorted with rage, yet laughing at the curse she was about to bestow, was alive in my mind. It was almost like a flashback to what she'd done to me back in ancient Greece – but this time I didn't see myself as her victim, I was seeing poor Arachne. How could Athena turn someone so good and kind into a spider?

With the image of Athena standing over the helpless Arachne in my mind, I sucked in an enormous breath and **SCREAMED**. The horrified faces in the audience told me that the other snakes were appearing. It was working! My scalp burned as my whole hair transformed into snakes, slithering round my head like flames dancing in a fire.

Inna stood up in the audience and started clapping. Others followed suit – first Cassandra,

then Echo and the other ancient Greeks – but soon the whole audience was on their feet.

A rumbling came from just outside the school. What was it going to be? Was a swarm of owls about to reappear and steal me back to ancient Greece? The rumbling grew louder and louder, and the ground started to tremble. The stage shifted. I stumbled back to the empty awards table and dropped Arachne.

I looked over to Hades' well. Jeremy was still standing there – or, at least, trying to stand there as the ground shifted beneath him. The sound grew louder and louder. And then suddenly it stopped. In the silence a large puff of dust blew out from the well – and that was it.

I put my hand up to my head – and felt hair! Glorious luscious curls! And there, under the awards table, was a very human, but

rather naked, Arachne. Thank
goodness for tablecloths!

I offered up a private
thanks to Hades. It turns out
he was trustworthy after
all.

As everyone got
back to their feet, Ms Williams approached the
microphone and said, "Thank you, Meddy, for
that ... um ... interesting performance."

Ms Williams tried to explain away the ground
shaking as a mini earthquake, but as she looked
over to where Hades' well had just imploded, she
caught sight of Jeremy. A dreamy look washed
across her face, and she made this bizarre growl
into the microphone. She even seemed to start
salivating.

Jeremy squealed and pelted in the direction
of home.

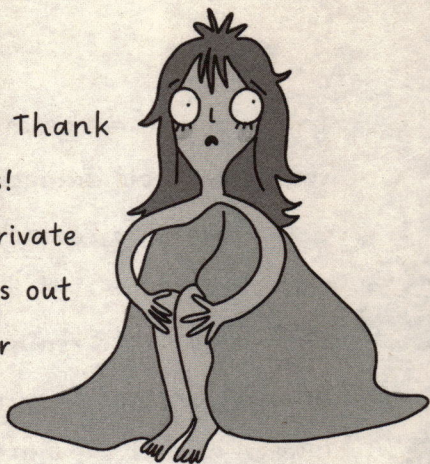

"Um, Ms Williams?" I spoke, trying to distract her. "What do we do now?"

She shook herself and snapped out of her trance. "That's it. Prize-giving is over. The term is over!" she called to the cheering crowd. "Happy holidays!"

Now that I'm staying in the twenty-first century, I guess there's even more stuff I need to learn about.

Number One: what's a holiday?

DATE:

Who cares? I'm on holiday.

TIME:

Who cares? Holiday time, baby!

Can you believe that schoolchildren here get **SIX WEEKS OFF SCHOOL?!** Six weeks! The more I think about that, the more I laugh at Hades tricking Athena into thinking that the twenty-first century is the most terrible place imaginable. And even the sun has come out for the holidays (just a little – we can't expect miracles, you know).

With so much free time stretching in front of me, there's no hurry to make plans, but I'm looking forward to doing more stuff with my new friends. Tomorrow, we've arranged a **"picnic"** with the other ancient Greeks – weather dependent, of course. But today, Inna, Arachne and I are catching a bus. A bus! I'm so excited. I never thought humans would ever be able to travel so fast. I'm really looking forward to my first bus ride. It will be utterly exhilarating. Gail and Tina were supposed to be coming with us, but they've been booked to make a celebrity appearance at a "department store" **(whatever that is)**, and they've taken Jeremy with them as "protection" against overenthusiastic fans.

So it's just the three of us. I'm so pleased that Inna and Arachne are getting on well.

Of course, Arachne is insisting on wearing all black, and when we can't find her, she's generally tucked away in some corner, or behind the sofa, but apart from that (and the odd fly-eating incident), her spideryness is firmly behind her. And she's still super good at weaving. Thankfully **NOT** butt weaving.

As for me, I am so relieved to be over the whole head-of-snakes thing. I do miss Mr Car and Ian, though. Isn't it strange what you can get used to? I did have one small panic this morning. When I woke up, there was a great big **SPOT** on my nose. I screamed in horror. Was Athena somehow still punishing me? Was this the start of me being turned into a repulsive monster? Gail and Tina reassured me that it's just my age. How do they know?

When they were my age, they were scaly sea monsters! They've provided me with twenty-seven different kinds of lotion, so hopefully my skin can remain beautifully clear and I will forever be Meddy Gordon, a normal fresh-faced twenty-first-century twelve-year-old girl.

Medusa Gorgon, terrifyingly hideous snake-haired creature that turns people to stone? Who's she?

Laters xx

THE END

EXODUS

Exodus? What does that mean?

The story's over. We get to leave the stage.

Aw. But I was enjoying that. I wanted to see someone being turned to stone!

Medusa is safe in the twenty-first century. She's fine now.

You think?

You don't?

Medusa has angered various gods. And what about Tantalus? He's back in ancient Greece, and he knows what Medusa's fate should have been. If he's evil enough to trick the gods into eating human flesh, I wonder what he might be tempted to do with information about Medusa. He's probably looking for Perseus right now. There's definitely **unfinished business**.

Oooh yes.

MORE! MORE!

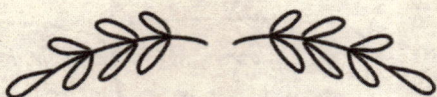

ACKNOWLEDGEMENTS

What? Am I supposed to **THANK** people in **MY** diary?

You do know I wrote it **ALL BY MYSELF?**

OK, fine.

I should definitely thank my awesome BFF Arachne, without whom I'd have never thought to write a diary (although, arguably, by giving me the diary idea, she started off the whole sequence of events that led to snake hair and everything else!).

Thanks to Inna for your friendship and understanding.

Thanks to my sisters, Gail and Tina, for helping me, and for showing me there is a way to make a different fate for myself.

Thanks to Sophie and the Os for teaching me what kind of person I'd rather not be (but it's fine if you want to be that person – you do you!)

Thanks to Jeremy for being lovely and gentle, and not a bloodthirsty monster.

Thanks to Hades for ... well, you know what you did. Isn't it great when people surprise you?

And thank you to YOU, my dear readers. I do hope you're not being too bothered by your **BOTTOM BOILS.**

What, do WE not get a thank you?

Charming!

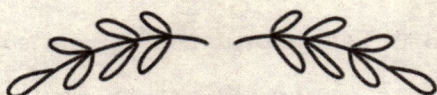

PROPER ACKNOWLEDGEMENTS

I'd like to start with a **MASSIVE THANK YOU** to Scholastic, and the utterly fantastic Lauren Fortune, for so enthusiastically taking on this story of a young Medusa, and allowing me to create an ancient Greek **TRAGEDY** in the form of a funny middle-grade book! **BUCKETLOADS** OF **THANKS** to Isabella Haigh, for excellent support and guidance through the whole process, and to many other marvellous people at Scholastic: Sarah Dutton, Wendy Shakespeare, Aimee Stewart, Hannah Love, Kiran Kharnom, Rosie Watts and Holly Clarke.

    A HUMUNGOUS THANK YOU goes to the super-talented Katie Abey, whose illustrations have brought Medusa's words and world to life in ways I could only dream of. And, of course, **MEGA THANKS** to Jo Williamson, my agent, who helped Medusa find her place in our world.

HUGE THANKS to my super-duper writing community, who all help make this strange job of sitting alone at a computer and making up stories feel not quite so strange or lonely! And **ENDLESS THANKS** go to my husband and children, for not minding me disappearing off to sit alone at a computer.

To help understand the trials, tribulations and annoyances for twelve-year-old girls, I drafted in some help. **THANK YOU** to Zoe, Lottie, Maddy, Rahma, Molly, Edie, Mabel, Mia, Leonie, Milo, Eden for your input. I hope this book reflects some of the things you shared, even if you didn't have to experience them as an ancient Greek character suddenly transported to the twenty-first century!

And thank you to my fabulous friends: Jenny, Lisa, Helen, Emily, Liz, Ines, Rachel, Holly, Kate, Anna and Lisette. You are all strong, independent, creative, funny and fantastic, and I am grateful for everything you bring to my life.

I have been wanting to write a story about Medusa for years. My love of Greek myths started around the age of ten, when I was given the *Usborne Illustrated Guide to Greek Myths and Legends*. It rapidly became my favourite-ever non-fiction book, and I have it to this day. In that book, the picture of Medusa is truly hideous, and her demise at the hands of Perseus is described, but **her** story is barely mentioned. That has been my inspiration for this story. So thank you to whoever gave me that book. It just goes to show that, if you want to have a positive impact on a child, give them a book!

ABOUT THE AUTHOR

BETHANY WALKER'S BAD HAIR DAY

Between the ages of ten and twenty, Bethany had a perm. It could be said that, instead of having a bad hair day, she had a **BAD HAIR DECADE**. Since ditching the perm, Bethany has gone on to be a teacher, a museum educator and, now, a writer of very funny children's books. Is this due to a change in hairstyle? Who can say?*

*Probably not. It's down to hard work, perseverance, a supportive family and, now, all the ridiculous ideas that keep coming out of Bethany's head.

ABOUT THE ILLUSTRATOR

KATIE'S TRIM-MENDOUS
RAINBOW HAIR

Katie and her hair have had quite the
journey over the years. From that time
when she was nine when she "trimmed"
her fringe and had a sticking-up bit
for months ... to her teen years when her
hair weekly made its way through every
shade of the rainbow. It has been through
a lot and has now finally ended up settling
as a bright yellow. Her sunshine hair is,
without a doubt, the source of her
art powers!

MAP OF SHADEWELL
(21ST CENTURY)

SHADEWELL ACADEMY

HADES' WELL

HOME
YARD